SHADOW-CATCHER

BETTY LEVIN

SHADOW-CATCHER

GREENWILLOW BOOKS

An Imprint of HarperCollins*Publishers*

The text of this book is set in Trump.

Library of Congress Cataloging-in-Publication Data
Levin, Betty.
Shadow-catcher / by Betty Levin.
p.   cm.
"Greenwillow Books."
Summary: Although he often fancied himself a detective,
Jonathan must become a real sleuth when he attempts to solve
a mystery while accompanying his grandfather, a Civil
War veteran and traveling photographer in Maine.
ISBN 0-688-17862-6
[1. Grandfathers—Fiction.   2. Photography—Fiction.
3. Mystery and detective stories.]   I. Title.
PZ7.L5759 Sh   2000
[Fic]—dc21   99–045087

10 9 8 7 6 5 4 3 2 1
First Edition

For Thomas Williamson

1

The Sunday Mrs. Miranda Noone appeared at church, a day that was to prove momentous because of what it sparked, Jonathan Capewell missed all the early signals that should have alerted a detective in training.

That was how he thought of himself: a detective like Wizard Will, the Boy Ferret of New York, or Fergus Fearnaught, the New York Boy, heroes of the fast-paced dime novels he read whenever he could.

Even though Jonathan had never set foot in any city, he could almost see the mean streets where sly criminals lurked. In his mind's eye he would close in on them like those young detectives. It didn't matter that he lived on a farm in northern Maine. He had only to spy an arrowhead in a freshly plowed field to imagine it a vital clue to a crime that he alone could solve.

No one but Jonathan's best friend, Warren, who supplied the detective stories, knew that every arrowhead Jonathan added to his collection served as a training trophy—just so long as Jonathan had discovered it himself.

But that spring Sunday he blundered along like a rabbit heading unaware for the snare that is set for it. To begin with, he was the last in his family to notice that Mrs. Noone and Grandpa seemed to be old friends. He did see that his sister, Rose, couldn't keep her eyes off Mrs. Noone's fashionable, lavender-scented traveling dress. He even heard Mama mistakenly call her Mrs. Moon, only to be corrected by Grandpa: "No, Sara, this is Mrs. Noone of Masham." When Mama tried to cover her confusion by remarking on the great distance Mrs. Noone had traveled, and all by herself, too, Jonathan still failed to detect the edge of disapproval in Mama's tone.

Grandpa said he would attend to Mrs. Noone's horse. It would have a good rest and feed in the village before she had to return to Masham. His family would make room in the wagon for her and for the photographic supplies she had brought him.

Jonathan just assumed that everyone was proud to receive such an elegant visitor. But appearances are distracting, if not downright deceiving. Even though detectives are supposed to have eagle eyes so that no detail escapes their notice, Jonathan didn't have an inkling about Mama's alarm until they were home in the parlor and she went all blotchy red. Jonathan found this bewildering. All he could tell was that Grandpa expected Mrs. Noone to stay to Sunday dinner.

Mama whispered to Grandpa that she needed some warning if she was to serve guests at her Sunday table. Grandpa replied that Miranda didn't need things gussied up for her. Then Mama fled to the kitchen, leaving the rest of the family tongue-tied and Mrs. Noone seated on the edge of the good chair, her hands folded and a stiff smile scoring her face.

When Mama called for Rose, Mrs. Noone asked if she could help, too. "I don't mean to put you out," she said. "Maybe I could—"

But Mama cut her short. "Thank you, no."

Mrs. Noone stood up, walked to Grandpa, placed one pale hand on his dark sleeve, and said, "Perhaps we should try this visit another time, when you can give your daughter-in-law some advance warning."

Looking embarrassed, Grandpa declared, "You're welcome here anytime. Isn't that right?" he demanded of Mama. "Sara, aren't my guests welcome in my house?"

Mama stepped out of the kitchen, her floured hands held out in front of her. "Yes, of course," she replied. "Your house," she repeated.

Mrs. Noone then said, "Thank you so much. This has been a pleasant visit, and I've stayed long enough." She moved toward the front hall, turned, and said, "I enjoyed meeting you all and seeing where Rodney lives when he's not in Masham."

"Did you hear that?" Mama asked after Grandpa had hitched up Teddy and driven away with Mrs. Noone. "She enjoyed seeing the house. I'll bet she did."

"Sara," Dad responded, "that was just manners."

Mama started to retort, then pressed her lips together before returning to the kitchen.

Later, as Sunday dinner drew to a close without Grandpa, Dad suggested setting a plate on the stove to keep warm.

Mama turned her indignation on Dad. "I don't need to be

instructed. Haven't I taken care of your father all these years?"

"Very well, Sara," Dad replied. "But don't forget that he's on the road a good many months and seeing to himself."

"Or being seen to," she retorted. Then she sighed. "Later," she said to him. "We'll speak of this later."

Even though she was talking to Dad, Jonathan caught the sweep of her glance. It was directed at him.

His brothers and sister applied themselves to the food on their plates. No one said another word until Mama asked Rose to fetch the pie.

Jonathan couldn't tell whether Mama had focused on him just because he was the youngest or for some other reason beyond his grasp. Maybe his brothers and sister understood why his parents were so stirred up over Grandpa's "friend." All Jonathan needed to do was ask them. It ought to be as simple as that.

2

Jonathan paused at the open door to the sewing room. It scarcely had space enough for Rose's bed as well as for the table where Mama laid out cloth. Still, Jonathan envied Rose this private space. She sat now with her back against the wall, a schoolbook on her knees.

"Grandpa's not home," he said.

Rose shrugged. "It's not yet dark."

"Will he be cross with Mama?"

Rose shrugged again.

Jonathan went out to the barn, where Simon was feeding the calves.

"Isn't this your job?" Simon asked him.

"It's early," Jonathan replied. "It's not yet dark," he thought to add.

Simon cast a look at Jonathan. Then he said, "Maybe you're not cut out for farming. Maybe you'll have to learn a trade instead. How would you like that?"

A trade? Did being a detective and catching robbers count as a trade? Jonathan doubted that Wizard Will or Fergus Fearnaught regarded their calling that way. He couldn't imagine any of his other dime novel heroes being in trade, not even Captain Coldgrip, the City Sleuth. "You mean," asked Jonathan, "like being a shoemaker or a shopkeeper?"

Simon straightened and fixed him with an odd look. "Or a camera man."

A photographer like Grandpa! Traveling through the countryside and staying in towns and visiting fairs and working with glass and smelly bottles of fluid that stained your fingers and your clothes. Jonathan didn't think he would like sleeping in a wagon full of all that equipment. Grandpa always made him keep his hands at his sides whenever he went near those trays and cases full of glass plates.

"I was going to feed the calves," he said. "I didn't forget to. I'll be a farmer."

Simon said, "Maybe. Maybe not."

What did he mean by that? "It's something about Mrs. Noone, isn't it?" Jonathan guessed. But why should it have anything to do with him?

Simon handed him two buckets and nodded him off in the direction of the well.

"If you and Albert know, why can't I?" Jonathan demanded.

"You're too young," Simon told him. "Anyway, you'll learn soon enough if—" He broke off.

"If what?" Jonathan pleaded. He felt all prickly, the way he did when something or someone seemed to be following him in the dark woods.

"If you're to go with Grandpa," Simon said. "But don't ask me for the whys and wherefores. If Mama wants you to know, she'll tell you."

Jonathan trudged out to the well. There he rinsed out the buckets, using the clean one kept only for bringing up water. He gazed all around. Leave this farm? His throat tightened. He knew no other place, except through schoolbooks and Grandpa's pictures. And the dime novels.

He had never been to even a small city or ridden on a train, and the only fair he knew was the one in Bridgetown, the nearest thing to a home fair. It was one thing to dream of outsmarting criminals on city streets, but quite another to be shunted from home. Thinking of traveling afar without brothers or sister, without parents, sent his thoughts reeling away from his head like so many weeds tossed from a scythe.

He carried the buckets back to the barn and then hesitated, hoping that Simon would reveal something more. When no words came, Jonathan spoke up. "Dad will need me for the haying."

Simon said, "We did without you when you were too little."

If Simon knew why Mrs. Noone had made Mama so cross, he wasn't saying. As far as Jonathan could tell, Grandpa's "friend" had been extremely polite. More than that, thoughtful. She had gone out of her way to bring Grandpa a crate full of equipment sent all the way from New York. It had been shipped to her home in Masham since it couldn't be mailed to the farm. Was that what troubled Mama?

Or did it have something to do with Mrs. Noone's fine dress and scent?

Just thinking about her made Jonathan's nose wrinkle at the remembered sweetness.

That night Jonathan lingered downstairs before going up to bed. Then, hoping to hear his family talking, he struggled to stay awake. But sleep crept up on him as it always did, even before his brothers joined him. In the morning they were already up and out to chores when his sister woke him.

He was mopping his plate with the last of his biscuit when Grandpa appeared in the kitchen. Mama heaped cornmeal mush and ham on a plate, ladled maple syrup over it, and set it in front of Grandpa with a thud.

Grandpa inclined his head. "Thank you, Sara," he said before reaching for a biscuit.

Mama said, "Jonathan, you'll be late for school."

So once again he was barred from knowing what this was all about. Still, he might pry some information out of Rose.

He pelted down to the road, caught up with her, and asked, "Why is Mama so cross with Grandpa?"

Rose let out a sigh.

"Please, it's not fair if everyone else knows, especially if I'm to go with him."

Rose stopped. "How do you— What makes you think that?" she asked him.

So it was true! "I know some things," he answered cagily. "But not the reasons."

Rose considered this for a moment. Even though they were alone on the road, she lowered her voice. "Mama is afraid that Grandpa might marry Mrs. Noone."

"Marry!" Jonathan exclaimed. "He's too old." Why would a pretty woman like Mrs. Noone marry a grandfather? "Besides, she's a missus already."

"She might be a widow," Rose told him. "Anyhow,

Mama's worried about losing the farm. Mrs. Noone might marry Grandpa to get his property."

Jonathan shook his head. Mrs. Noone didn't look anything like a farmer's wife, even though she had driven her own buggy a long way. "Why would she want the farm?" he asked. "Grandpa doesn't even care about it."

"That's right. That's what Mama says. He never did care. She says it was always run-down when Dad was growing up. Dad's own grandparents mostly raised him after his mother died, even before his father went south to be a soldier in the war. After Grandpa was wounded and came home, he worked some, but he paid scant attention to farm matters. Mama says if it weren't for Dad, there would be no living off it now. As for Mrs. Noone, Mama says some women just call themselves missus to look respectable, especially when they're not."

"Mrs. Noone isn't respectable?" asked Jonathan.

Ahead on the road Ethel and Carrie Woodstock waited for them.

"Not one word of this in front of them," Rose warned.

"Just tell what isn't respectable," he implored.

"I can't," Rose whispered. "Not now." Then, in spite of her resolve, she added, "Mrs. Noone travels alone. She runs a business and has city ways." Then Rose clammed up. A moment later she was chatting with Ethel and Carrie.

What did Rose mean by city ways? Jonathan wondered. How could he find out?

3

The week settled into its usual routine. It was almost as if nothing had actually happened. Or would happen. Dad and the boys finished the plowing and were seeding. Rose and Jonathan had school first and then farm chores afterward. No one mentioned Mrs. Noone.

Grandpa readied his wagon and equipment for the summer's photography circuit. He was his customary self, quiet and agreeable. And remote.

Jonathan did his best to overhear conversations carried on behind doors, but even when he heard his own name mentioned, he couldn't make anything of it.

So he was taken by surprise on Saturday night when Mama called him into the kitchen at bath time. Most Saturdays he was the last one into the copper tub, when the water was almost cold. But this time he was ahead of his brothers. Steam rose, the water already soapy from Rose's and Mama's use.

"Scrub well," Mama ordered as she fastened her nightdress and collected his discarded clothes. "Head and all."

Slowly Jonathan folded himself into the hot water, drawing his knees almost to his chin. It felt so good he dreaded getting out. Filling the dipper, he squeezed his eyes shut and then sloshed soapy water over his head. Mama reappeared with a fresh nightshirt. She eyed him critically.

"Scrub," she said again before leaving him.

He tried to sink lower. The water slopped up. Quick as anything he jumped out of the copper, reached for the rag mop, and wiped up the spill. Shivering, he grabbed the flannel, already wet from Rose, and hugged it around himself for a moment before slipping on his nightshirt. He would have hovered for a moment beside the woodstove, but Simon was telling him to shake a leg and Mama was calling down to him to take himself into the parlor.

There he waited, growing cold and anxious, certain now that something was afoot. When his parents and his grandfather came in, he knew at once that whatever they had decided was fixed, beyond appeal. He began to shiver.

"Bring the boy into the kitchen," Dad said.

"They're still bathing," Mama said.

"What of it? It's no secret. They all know."

"All but Jonathan," Grandpa remarked. "The oldest and the youngest, the last to know."

"Now, Father," Mama responded, "you said you didn't object."

Without replying, Grandpa stared at Jonathan, commanding him silently to return his gaze.

"Your grandfather wants to bring you along with him," Mama said.

Grandpa said nothing.

Jonathan looked into Grandpa's weathered face. It was composed; it revealed nothing. The eyes were a striking blue, the shaggy eyebrows a dark contrast with the white, trimmed beard. As far back as Jonathan could remember, Grandpa had lived apart, even when he was among them. He had never shown more than a kind of genial affection for his youngest grandson. And now he wanted Jonathan?

"I was your age when your grandfather joined the Union army," Dad told Jonathan. "My grandparents carried on here with me, as they had since Mother died. During those war years I began to be a help to them." Dad paused. He seemed to be choosing his words with care. "And now you're old enough to begin to help your grandfather. And to learn about taking pictures. You ought to pick up the skill quick enough, considering how well you do in school."

"It's an opportunity to improve yourself," Mama said. "So when your grandfather becomes . . . less able to do everything, we can count on you to watch out for him."

Still Grandpa didn't speak. His look held Jonathan's.

"So you must try hard," Dad said.

"Be good," Mama added.

"When?" asked Jonathan.

"In a few days," Mama said. "I have to mend for the two of you before you go."

"What about school?" Jonathan said.

"It's almost let out," Dad reminded him. "You'll have a longer summer holiday, that's all. You can catch up next fall."

"Won't I come home at all?" Jonathan asked, trying hard to keep his voice level.

"That's up to your grandfather," Mama told him.

Jonathan swallowed. "I've never been away from home."

"It's not as though you were going off on your own," Dad told him.

"It's a wrench, though," Grandpa said. "As I recall, first time I went, I was scared of my own shadow, and I was a grown man."

"But that was for the war. You were going into battle," Dad said. "You had reason to be afraid."

Grandpa shook his head. "It was bad like that before I ever heard a shot fired. Everything strange. Not knowing anyone."

Jonathan clutched himself to quiet the shivering.

"Then it's settled," Mama said. "Now, Jonathan, get to bed and warm up."

Jonathan had a feeling that she wanted to end this conversation before Grandpa said anything more to scare him off.

4

Jonathan still couldn't figure out why he was picked. To help Grandpa? How could he be helpful when Grandpa didn't seem to need or want help? To stop Mrs. Noone from marrying Grandpa? What could Jonathan do about it? He didn't know a thing about city ways, unless they were reflected in the Low Life on Mean Streets described in dime novels. Where did Mrs. Noone fit into that setting?

After school on Monday he raised this question with Warren, whose uncle kept them supplied with discarded dime novels that he brought home from the railroad.

Warren used to prefer cowboy stories until his favorite hero moved east and turned detective in *Cool Colorado in New York, or the Cowboy's Fight for a Million: A Romance of City and Wild West.* "You've read more about city life than I have," Warren said to Jonathan. "Don't some stories mention Fancy Ladies?"

Jonathan nodded. "But what do they do, and why would Grandpa be friends with one? And how can I stop her?"

Warren was stumped. "Are you sure she comes from a city?"

Jonathan shook his head. Masham was a town, the biggest and busiest for many miles around. But no one called it a city. As far as he knew, Grandpa mostly traveled around taking pictures for weddings and family reunions and special events like baseball games and fairs so that he could afford to take all the other photographs for his own pleasure.

Warren sighed. "And you'll be gone all summer?"

Jonathan nodded. He wouldn't mind missing the hard, boring work, hoeing and picking vegetables and haying. But the long summer included swimming and treasure hunting and tree climbing, too. Jonathan and Warren had always done these together.

After school Mama made Jonathan try on clothes she had altered. Only the sleeves of Simon's patched jacket still needed to be turned up. "Just remember," she said, "you can't be snagging on brambles and scraping yourself rock climbing. If there are any new holes or rips while you're on the road, you'll have to make do."

"Grandpa stitches harness leather," Jonathan said. "He fixes shoes, too."

Mama sniffed. She didn't think that kind of sewing counted.

But that night, when Jonathan went upstairs to bed, she came to his room. Standing just inside the door, she said, "You'll be careful now, won't you?"

"Yes," he said. "Careful of what?"

"It will be a good lesson for you," she continued without responding.

"A photography lesson?" he asked.

"Yes. It might prepare you for a different sort of life." Then she added, "Though you're young to be gone from your family."

Maybe she would relent and keep him home. He held his breath.

"True, your grandfather is family," she added. "But all these years he hasn't always acted that way, especially with all his coming and going, sometimes away for months on end, doing goodness knows what—"

"Wasn't he taking pictures?" Jonathan asked.

"Of course. But that can't occupy a grown man all the time. I'm sure I don't know what he's about. Your dad says the war turned him in on himself. But that was long ago. He's never taken to proper farming since." She broke off, walked over to the bed, and sat down beside Jonathan. "You will take care, won't you?" she said.

Jonathan nodded. He wasn't at all sure what she was saying. She had almost seemed worried on his account until her talk veered around to Grandpa. Now she spoke of Grandpa when Jonathan needed to hear about Mrs. Noone. When would Mama explain what Jonathan must do to keep Mrs. Noone from getting the farm?

"Be with Grandpa always," she continued. "Watch out for him."

"Why?" Jonathan asked her. "He's used to being on his own when he goes off picture taking. He's always fine."

"He's older now," Mama said. She leaned forward, her voice low. "Sometimes people grow a bit foolish as they age. So promise me you'll look out for him. Promise, son."

Jonathan nodded. Why wouldn't she speak of Mrs. Noone? How exactly was he supposed to protect Grandpa? Were there certain signs of foolishness he should be on the lookout for?

Or was Mama hinting that Grandpa was foolish already?

5

When Jonathan climbed inside the wagon with his pack of clothes, Grandpa merely nodded toward a shelf below the folding worktable. Jonathan had managed to roll up two dime novels and insert them into the pack. Grandpa paid scant attention to those belongings and little more to Jonathan himself.

Jonathan had pleaded with Simon for direction. "What am I supposed to do?" he had whispered. "Tell me what to do."

Simon had shaken his head. "I'm not sure. I guess he'll be seeing to you. You being with him all the time, not just to learn photography, that may put the lady off."

"Does Grandpa mind having me?" Jonathan had asked.

Simon had tried to shrug off the question. "Maybe. You know how Grandpa likes his independence. I mean, even when he's here, you always get the feeling his mind is somewhere else. Still, he might come to enjoy teaching you how to take pictures."

There were last-minute additions to the wagon: two loaves of bread, a tin of biscuits, jars of jam, a jug of syrup, and smoked pork. Even though Jonathan had eaten a big breakfast, seeing and smelling all that food made him hungry. How long before they would stop for dinner?

"Promise you'll look out for him," Mama called as Grandpa gathered up the reins.

Grandpa nodded, and at the same time Jonathan, seated beside him, said, "Yes, Mama."

Grandpa shot a quick glance at him, then clucked to Teddy, who started forward with a lurch. His gait was stiff as he held back on the steep track to the road, but as soon as the wagon turned onto the gentler downhill slope, he eased up and trotted forward with spirit.

Jonathan looked back along the side of the wagon where pails and sacks of tools and feed were hung. It reminded him of the peddler cart that visited the farm once or twice a year with pots and pans and jars and paraffin and fabric and needles and scissors and combs and cocoa and coffee and tea and lamps. You could hear that cart clattering up the road long before you saw it. But everything on Grandpa's wagon was snug and tight. All the breakables were fastened inside and crammed on shelves Grandpa had built just for them.

For a while the way was familiar. Grandpa slowed to greet neighbors whenever they passed farms. Once he stopped to let Teddy drink from the brook that ran beside the road, but he didn't invite Jonathan to get down, and he didn't mention food. So Jonathan just sat and listened to the rushing water and the clank of the bit rings and the persistent bellowing of a cow he couldn't see. He wondered if Warren and the others were eating their lunches now. If so,

Jonathan's brothers would be coming in to sit with Dad and Mama in the warm kitchen for their midday meal.

Or maybe it wasn't yet noon. How could time be measured or even guessed at when nothing happened to mark the divisions of the day? Jonathan ached from sitting so long; his stomach clenched with anxiety.

On they went. Grandpa seemed to have some destination in mind. Only where the road was rutted from snowmelt did he slow Teddy to a walk. Then finally, when the uphill climb grew steep, he stopped and beckoned Jonathan down.

Jonathan's knees almost buckled. He staggered, then gripped the shaft. Grandpa was running his hand over Teddy's back. At last he spoke. "He could do with a break."

Grandpa found a stone to block the rear wheel and nodded at Jonathan, who went in search of another one for the wheel on his side. Then he helped Grandpa unhitch Teddy and remove the bit. Traces had to be looped, the reins draped and caught around the hames. Then Grandpa gave Teddy a slap to let him know he was free to browse. Teddy shook himself hard. He dropped his head and began to strip new leaves from blackberry canes. When he came across a stand of goldenrod, not yet in bud, first he nibbled the young leaves, and then he gobbled the entire plants, stalks and all.

Grandpa clambered into the wagon and emerged with a loaf, hard-boiled eggs, and a jug of water. Lunch was only one slice of bread and one egg apiece. When Jonathan had finished his and was hoping for more, Grandpa said, "We'll be walking awhile. It's hard going; you don't want to be climbing uphill on a full stomach." And he put the bread away in the wagon.

When Teddy was back between the shafts and bitted and hitched once more, Grandpa slid his hand under the collar and harness, rubbing where the horse had sweated, just feeling for trouble spots. Then he nodded and bent to remove the stone block. On Jonathan's side the stone was so tightly wedged that he couldn't budge it until Teddy stepped forward.

Then they set off, Grandpa walking beside the horse, Jonathan to the side until the road became so steep that he had trouble keeping up. After a while he simply followed. It was dusty behind the wagon, and he had to watch out for small stones kicked up by the wheels.

A whole summer like this? He couldn't imagine why he had been condemned to such misery. How was he supposed to keep Mrs. Noone away from Grandpa or to help him when he couldn't even keep up with him? How was he to learn about photography from this old man who wouldn't even speak to him?

Besides, there wasn't a sign of Mrs. Miranda Noone, and the last thing Jonathan could imagine was Grandpa's perfectly garbed "friend" trudging up a mountain road that seemed to lead nowhere at all.

6

There was nothing to break the monotony of the days on the road, nothing to ease the nights in the cramped wagon with a snoring old man. Never once did Grandpa mention where they were heading. Jonathan wanted to know, but Grandpa's silence kept him from asking. He felt hungry most of the time and cold some of the time and lonely all of the time.

When Grandpa stopped to take a picture, first he set up his tripod and camera, next he coated a glass negative plate, and then he took a long time focusing, waiting for a certain kind of light. Sometimes after all that preparation he didn't even make a photograph. If this was the working of an addled mind, Jonathan couldn't imagine what he could do about it.

As the roads worsened, sometimes a wheel got mired, and then both man and boy had to get behind the wagon to push while Teddy strained to haul it free. Often they had to get down just to lighten the load. Jonathan began to look forward to walking simply because it was a change.

Once in a while they met up with people, and while

Grandpa asked directions, Jonathan let himself believe that they would soon arrive somewhere, be somewhere. Then, after two full days of nothing but trees and mosquitoes, new sounds finally reached Jonathan's ears.

Teddy's pace picked up. Jonathan raised his eyes. One sweeping glance showed him a changed landscape. On either side of the road the earth looked scarred, the trees gone, but with no meadowland in their place. Soon occasional voices came through, the rattle of chains, and, once, a tremendous crash that shook the ground and set off a shrill alarm of birds.

Grandpa turned Teddy onto a byroad. The horse's ears pricked forward over his black forelock. Raising his muzzle, he neighed. Ahead of them another horse answered.

Grandpa said, "Easy, boy."

Jonathan knew he was speaking to the horse. He felt like saying, "What about me?"

They moved forward, Grandpa on one side of Teddy's head, Jonathan on the other. First only smoke was visible. Then, suddenly, there were log shelters, a fenced yard, horses, and men.

One man looked up. "Rod?" Then he called to someone, "It's Rod Capewell."

Others came forward.

"We figured you weren't going to make it this year."

"That's one way to put it," a man remarked. "We wondered if you'd died."

"Who's this?" another asked, nodding at Jonathan.

"Youngest grandson," Grandpa replied. "Supposed to learn about picture taking."

"We expected you a month ago."

"Roads too soft for wheels," Grandpa said.

The others nodded agreement. This year the snow had hung on everywhere.

"I hoped to make it for the first river drive," Grandpa said.

"The next one's about to start, but there're logjams still to be cleared and not enough hands," one of them told him. "It's been a rough winter. Accidents and that."

Teddy was set loose in the fenced yard. He pawed the hard ground, swung his head low, folded his knees, and dropped down to roll. After he jumped up and shook himself, bits of hay and dirt still stuck to his brown hair. Grandpa told Jonathan to wash him and scrub hard at the sweat marks from the harness, especially where the surcingle sometimes caked the hair on his belly. Someone handed Jonathan a bucket of water and a rag and left him to it.

Hay was thrown over the fence for Teddy. It looked so gray and weathered that Jonathan kicked it loose to make sure it wasn't moldy. Grandpa brought clean water.

As soon as Teddy was settled, Grandpa rummaged inside the wagon and emerged with the pork. Everyone crowded around to get a whiff of the smoky aroma. One of them said, "We've been heavy on muskrat stew since the ice started breaking up. This Indian fella, Muskrat Mac, he sings to the muskrats and then takes as many as he can carry. Now this piece of meat will be some good eating for a change. Cookee will dole it out." Another man told Grandpa to keep some for his travels, and he cut off one thick chunk to put away in the wagon.

Jonathan didn't dare remind him that there were two mouths to feed on the road. By now the meat had vanished, only its tantalizing smell lingering in the evening air. Jonathan followed Grandpa, staggering more from fatigue than from hunger. Still, when he heard that the men had already had their supper, his heart sank.

He barely listened to the talk that passed between Grandpa and the loggers. They were seated now, some on the ground, some on stumps or kegs. Grandpa had fetched a photograph from the wagon and presented it to a short, bowlegged man he called Cookee. As the picture was handed around, the men commented on their own likenesses and on images of those who were absent.

"You're a small group this year," Grandpa remarked.

"And we're late," Cookee said. "We've had a terrible lot of snow. The ice was a month or so late breaking up. The new foreman, sent out here to speed up production, talks pretty and listens to no one. He's always cutting corners and taking risks, like setting dynamite to the ice to speed the logs along on the river. You should see the floods we got."

Grandpa looked around.

"You won't see him here," Cookee said. "He's over to the east shore of Fish Hawk Lake now. We're moving camp to that side of the lake."

"Those of us that don't quit first," another man remarked. "By the time everything's moved, there won't hardly be any crew left."

"It's nobody's fault we're behind schedule," someone else explained. "It's the late season. But this boss, he thinks we hold back."

Grandpa said, "He must know you've been logging together for years."

"He doesn't care. He's after quick fixes. Often as not they're mantraps. Most of us know enough to steer clear of his schemes, so he looks for the man at the bottom or the youngest. Just now it's Mac Nichols, the Indian we call Muskrat Mac. He used to log up to St. John, so he knows enough to refuse the craziest risks. Doesn't matter who it is, though, there's bad feeling, and we won't get our pay until the job's finished."

The voices droned on around Jonathan like a swarm of sluggish bees. He was barely aware of the spoon and dish placed upon his crossed legs. Slowly the steam from hot beans and corn bread rose to his face. Someone set down a hot mug for him.

Looking across the circle of men, he saw Grandpa shoveling food into his mouth. Jonathan dug in. It tasted delicious. The mug contained sweetened tea, too hot to gulp, so he ate some more. Once again he tried the tea. He could feel it scald him as it went down. Never mind. Never mind anything. He had a bellyful of food. Nothing else mattered.

He was dimly aware of being picked up, of being deposited on a mat or floor and covered with a blanket. It was dark now, and he was warm and full. Maybe if he played dead, he could stay this way forever.

7

Jonathan awoke befuddled. He was in a crude lean-to, surrounded by blanket rolls and bulky gunnysacks hanging from nails. Boots upended on sticks leaned this way and that around a stove. The upside-down boots reminded him of late-fall sunflowers, their stems bent under heavy, ragged heads. But this lean-to didn't smell like any garden. It reeked of sweat and dirt, worse than Mama's kitchen on washday.

He was fully dressed. All he had to do was thrust off the blanket and get up. Except that his stiff legs took some arranging. Cookee poked his head inside, watched for a moment, and then told Jonathan where the privy was and where to come for breakfast.

When Jonathan made his way into the cook shed, no one else was there. On the long table he found a solitary spoon and a plate of corn bread, dried apple slices, and ham. He sat on the bench and regarded the food. He wasn't really hungry yet. But if Grandpa was getting ready to take to the road, Jonathan supposed he'd better eat everything in sight.

He heard voices outside. He heard hammering. He heard

crows and horses stomping and the sound of someone splitting wood.

Stuffed and thirsty, he caught sight of a barrel with a dipper lying on its heavy cover. Guessing right, he helped himself to a dipper of water. He saved a bit to slosh over the plate, which he finished wiping clean on his shirtsleeve.

Grandpa and Teddy were gone. For a moment he wondered if he had been left behind. For another moment he tried to figure out how that felt. Was he abandoned or spared? Then he saw the wagon. He went to it and climbed inside. He saw at once that the big camera and the tripod were gone, and probably a case of glass plates.

Outside again he spoke to a man dismantling a shed and stacking the notched logs. Had he noticed what direction Grandpa had set off in? The man said he was pretty sure Rod had headed for the river, below the lake where they were getting ready to release a great boom of logs for a run downstream. "You ever seen river logging before?" the man asked. "This'll be a wild one. When the water's this high and the current's running hard, only the best river drivers can hold their footing on the logs and keep them from piling up."

"I've never seen a big run," Jonathan said. "I guess I'll try to catch up with my grandfather and watch it."

"No, you wait here in camp," the man said. "You don't know your way, and you could miss him easy. Besides, I don't think they're starting just yet."

So Jonathan wandered about until Cookee gave him a job cleaning out the barrack stove. By the time he was finished shoveling the ashes, he was gray from head to toe.

"You growing fur?" one of the men asked as Jonathan lugged the bucket of ashes to the privy.

When Grandpa returned to camp, leading Teddy packed with photograph equipment, he made Jonathan undress and scrub down, clothes and all. But he wouldn't let Jonathan fetch anything dry from the wagon. "Save the clean clothes for town," he said. "Wrap yourself in a blanket until your things dry. Don't scorch them on the stove, though."

Later, while Jonathan huddled close to the kitchen fire, Cookee said, "Your grandfather seems out of sorts. Usually he keeps us entertained telling about all the people he's met on his journeys."

Jonathan said, "He doesn't talk much at home."

"No, well . . ." Cookee seemed to be considering. Then he added, "There's only one subject you won't hear him talk on, and that's the war. There're a few men who went south like him back in the sixties, but if they get started on those terrible battles, your grandfather, he just takes himself off."

Jonathan had never once heard Grandpa talk about the war. All he knew was that after Grandpa was wounded and a photographer took his picture, that was when Grandpa began to learn about cameras.

Cookee continued. "We see him most every spring. This is the first time he's seemed restless like this and broody."

Jonathan thought awhile. "It might be having me along," he said. "Grandpa doesn't talk to me."

"Aren't you with him to study on pictures?"

"It wasn't his idea," Jonathan said, thinking back to Mrs. Noone's visit.

Cookee grunted. He turned Jonathan's clothes to dry the other side.

Grandpa had hitched Teddy to a tree with hay and water. He said he would be going off tomorrow before dawn to catch the morning light on the river.

"Eat hearty tonight," Cookee told Jonathan. "Stoke up. Your grandpa moves right along."

"He can stay here," Grandpa said. "Give him something useful to do."

"Right you are, Rod," Cookee declared. "I guess peeling potatoes or scaling fish teaches a boy a deal of picture taking."

Grandpa stomped out to Teddy, but Cookee went after him, and they stayed away for a spell. Even after Cookee had returned to the kitchen shelter, Grandpa kept himself busy outside until Cookee banged a frypan and everyone in camp drifted in for the evening meal.

8

When Grandpa shook Jonathan awake, it seemed like the middle of the night. Jonathan shivered his way into his clothes and hurried outside. Maybe something exciting was about to happen. Stealing off like this while everyone else slept was the sort of thing a spy or a sleuth would have to do, passing unnoticed and in secret to surprise his quarry.

Grandpa carried the tripod and the breakables from the wagon. He entrusted Jonathan with bread and with one bulky pack. After loading everything on Teddy, Grandpa struck off into the darkness as though he could see. Teddy followed along, surefooted and calm. Once or twice Jonathan stumbled over a root or stone.

"You get used to it," Grandpa said. "Teddy and I, we've been tramping these woods together a number of years."

Thanks to Cookee, thought Jonathan, Grandpa sounded as though he was actually thawing. Afraid of making him frost up again, Jonathan didn't reply.

On they went, until at last dim gray light filtered through

the trees. Here and there patches of snow stood out from the dark ground.

Morning broke all at once, with a clamor. Unseen creatures on the ground and in the trees made such a racket that Jonathan was slow to hear a distant crashing that gradually overwhelmed the closer rustling and twitters and screeches and the creak and slap of leather against the surcingle that went around Teddy's middle like a belt.

As Grandpa led the horse between standing trees and blowdowns, Jonathan scooted off to one side and then the other. In front of him a wall of mist rose up and thickened, enveloping them in a moist chill.

"Slow down," Grandpa told him. "You're almost to the cliff."

Jonathan stopped. He'd often seen mist suspended over valleys on mornings like this. He'd never seen a cliff. He took one careful step after another, his hands thrust forward as if to push back the wall that seemed to block him. Then the ground dropped away. He turned back to Grandpa. "What is it?" he asked. "What's there?"

"The river," Grandpa said, tethering Teddy to a tree. "When the mist lifts, you'll see the rapids below, over there to your right. Straight down and to the left you'll see clear, fast water until the logs on Fish Hawk Lake are released from their boom. I was over that way yesterday. You can't see very far upriver from here. But I chose this spot because I want pictures before the logs shoot onto this course, as well as after, when they start coming, and after that when the river is all logs and they hit the rapids."

Jonathan peered down into the clammy baffle, that gray wall of moisture that blotted out the world below. There was nothing to see, nothing.

Grandpa loaded himself up with some of Teddy's pack. Jonathan stood by, waiting to be given something to do. "Should I carry something?" he asked finally.

Grandpa glanced at him. "Everything's breakable," he said. "Including you. You'll need your hands as well as your feet to keep your balance."

Grandpa descended sideways, leaning away from the weight of his equipment and against the steep slope. Jonathan was good at this kind of climbing on snowy hills. But here the drop was abrupt, the leaf mold underfoot surprisingly slick. Also the blinding mist was eerie, especially with that constant roar down below.

Grandpa stopped behind a granite outcrop and slid the tripod from his shoulder. Next came the box of glass plates, which he propped up with care before setting down the camera. He tramped back and forth, getting a feel of the solid ground beneath the dense layers of dead leaves and pine needles and rotting wood. He seemed to know exactly what he was looking for.

But did he? After all this careful preparation Grandpa sat himself down, pulled from his pack a chunk of bread, gave half to Jonathan, leaned back against a tree, and closed his eyes.

What now? wondered Jonathan, beginning to feel discouraged. Was this all they were going to do? After launching into what seemed like a real conversation, was Grandpa just going to sleep away the morning?

9

At first time itself seemed suspended in the sodden air. Then a warm breath stirred. It sent a ripple of light through the gray atmosphere. As soon as the mist thinned, time began to move again, its progress barely detectable, like an echo from an unheard voice.

Jonathan felt soft rays of sun on his face, on his head and shoulders. The rippled mist thinned some more, glistening as it dissolved. Far below, the river ran black and shiny as satin ribbon.

For a while Jonathan caught only glimpses of it. But as the sun rose, boulders rimmed with foam broke the swirling surface. Then, just where the river grew more turbulent, the mist gathered again. No, not mist, Jonathan realized. This was spray, spray that leaped high above the surface. He was looking at the rapids.

Not only at raging water but at a man as well and something else, dark above the white foam. Did Grandpa see this, too? He was behind the tripod and camera, sliding a glass plate into place. But he didn't say anything or even point. He drew a black cloth over his head and part of the camera. He waited.

Jonathan stepped aside and then climbed downward. He could see that the man, doubled over, was lunging at the thing, which seemed to be stuck between rocks and logs. The man crouched on a boulder to shift the logs with a long pole. His trousers and even his checked shirt were getting soaked. He managed to send one log and then another hurtling out into the current and down the rapids. Yet even after he had slid from the boulder into the water, he still failed to pry the other thing loose.

Scrambling lower, Jonathan craned for a closer look. All at once he realized that the thing was an overturned boat. Glancing back, he was about to shout to Grandpa when he saw him swivel the camera to aim upriver. Could Grandpa tell that the logs were coming?

Jonathan looked where the camera looked. But what came sweeping around the bend was no raft of logs. At first glance it looked like a small house. Or was it just a roof? It snagged on something, tipped, and then righted itself as it twirled and was checked yet again. Riding on top, its wings flapping, was a bedraggled rooster. Jonathan hoped Grandpa was taking a picture of this amazing sight before the roof broke up on the rocks.

Scanning the direction it was heading, Jonathan caught sight of another man on the far riverbank hauling a gunnysack down to the water. Jonathan looked for the man trying to dislodge the boat, but he saw no one, and the boat was gone. Was the man with the sack the same one who had struggled with the boat? Yes, even though his drenched clothes looked black, it was just possible to recognize that checked shirt.

The gunnysack, which he seemed to want in the river, resisted his efforts almost as much as the boat had. Every time it hooked on to something in its path, he yanked desperately and kicked it free. Jonathan could see the man's frantic gestures, his head jerking, his hair and beard whipping back and forth. He was in such a frenzy that he was going to miss the amazing sight of the waterborne roof and its solitary passenger.

"Look!" Jonathan shouted toward him. "Look what's coming!"

The crashing rapids must have drowned out his voice, because the man kept on dragging and backing until he maneuvered his burden onto a sloping rock at the water's edge and gave one mighty shove. The bulky gunnysack rolled over and over. Then the roof hurtled by, blocking Jonathan's view and claiming all his attention.

When the roof reached the rapids, it lumbered over one or two obstacles before it stopped, stranded in the middle of the churning current.

The man on the riverbank wasn't finished. He slipped and stumbled toward the roof, probing from the river's edge with the long pole that was tipped with a hook.

Looking around, Grandpa caught sight of the man on the rocks. "Fool!" Grandpa shouted. "He'll get himself drowned."

Jonathan called back to Grandpa, "Maybe he's trying to save the rooster."

Grandpa reached for another glass plate. "More likely

trying to clear the way for the logs, so they don't jam up in that splintering mess," he said.

The frenzy of stabbing and shoving went on long after the gunnysack had disappeared. Grandpa must be right. The man was clearing the way.

It took awhile for the river to beat the roof to smithereens. Struts and beams held out the longest against the terrific force of the water smashing it over the rocks.

Grandpa had already turned his camera upriver again when the terrified rooster flew at the man, who was still precariously balanced at the edge of the rapids. The man ducked and swung up a hand to fend it off. Only instead of fending, the man struck the flapping bird a swift blow that sent it down and out of sight.

He was still there, even after most of the roof had been carried off, when the first logs and men, along with two boats, appeared from upriver. The boats were hauled ashore before they were swept onto the rapids, but some of the men ran the logs that hurtled toward the savage plunge.

Jonathan thought the embattled man would be relieved to see that help was on its way. But when he finally noticed the oncoming logs, for one split second he simply gaped at what the river was shooting at him. Then his own peril made him quick. First staggering, he leaped out of the way and scrambled up the bank.

Grandfather slid a glass plate into its holder and shoved another into the camera. For the next few minutes he concentrated on picture taking, while the river below him was transformed into a massive stream of logs, and more men appeared to prod them on their wild course.

10

Back in camp Grandpa told Jonathan to be ready for another early start the following day.

"Won't you make the pictures first?" Jonathan asked. The roof had come too suddenly and then had begun to break up before he was able to take it all in. He was eager to see what the camera showed.

Grandpa shook his head. "In the old days it had to be done right off like that. But now I can print when it's easier, when we get to town. You want to learn how it's done?"

Jonathan didn't try to explain that what interested him was not the process but the results. It had been thrilling to watch the river drivers in their red shirts averting log-jams. They seemed more adept at their work than the man in the checked shirt had been. But of course they worked together, applying their poles, which Grandpa called pea-veys, with strength and precision. Sooner or later Jonathan would get to see those river pictures. Meanwhile his own impressions were freshly stored inside his head.

Grandpa told him to let Teddy go in the yard, then clean

him off so he'd be ready for the harness first thing in the morning.

Cookee leaned over the railing. "So did Rodney ease up on you some?" he asked.

Jonathan nodded. "He talked to me. We saw a roof on the river. There was a rooster on top."

"We're having a big fish fry tonight, but I could use a rooster. Why didn't you bring it back?"

"It flew the other way," Jonathan said. "A man hit it."

"I hope he bagged it. I expect we'll hear about it by and by," Cookee added. "Those rivermen like to add a touch of color to their stories before they tell us."

"Did you ever see a whole barn roof float on the river?"

Cookee shook his head. "Can't say as I did. It's not your everyday sight. I expect it's off the north shore of Fish Hawk Lake. I heard that after the ice was blown up and the water rose, some farm buildings over to that side got flooded out."

"Grandpa took pictures of it."

"What did you do?" Cookee asked.

"Stayed out of the way."

Cookee grinned. "That's some kind of start then. You'll be fine." He stumped off.

Jonathan wondered if Cookee was going to give Grandpa another talking-to, but it turned out he was simply asking if Grandpa could take tintypes for some of the loggers.

The group picture was made first. Grandpa told Jonathan to stand behind the camera and hold up a frypan for everyone to focus on. "Look!" Grandpa commanded from beneath the black cloth.

"Give us something worth looking at," one of the men retorted. "For eyes front, try a picture of a pretty woman."

The iron pan was so heavy, Jonathan had to prop it up with both hands.

Grandpa emerged from beneath the cover. "Should we wait?" he asked. "Will more of the men be back before dark?"

One of them said, "Not unless they find Muskrat Mac."

"They won't find him," someone else remarked. "He was sent to clear the backlogs," he explained to Grandpa. "It was an awful mess, too dangerous for one man. But the boss wouldn't let a proper crew off work to help."

"Maybe Mac didn't want that dirty job," said the first speaker, "but he went."

The second man shook his head. "He had his gear bag with him. He was fixing to head out."

"Not without his pay," a third man declared. "He's got a winter's wages coming."

Grandpa reset the camera. He took his time shooting the picture. Jonathan's arms trembled. Afterward, when he tried to lower the pan, he nearly dropped it. He was grateful that no one seemed to notice. The men were already lining up for tintype photographs. They didn't realize that Grandpa had to put away his glass plate and cumbersome camera and bring out different equipment.

Jonathan lugged the frypan back to the kitchen shelter and then went to watch the picture taking. Grandpa used the small camera with several lenses that he took to village picnics and church events. It allowed him to snap one picture after another. Back in the wagon they were developed on a thin metal sheet and hung out to dry.

Jonathan had never been allowed to stand so close before. "I thought you couldn't get a picture all at once," he said.

"These are really negatives," Grandpa told him. "The black backing makes them look like prints."

The men stared at the emerging images. When all the portraits were ready and cut apart, they were passed from hand to hand as if they were rare gems. Several of the men came forward with coins, but Grandpa refused payment.

"Maybe next time there'll be enough of you to make it worth my while," he told them. Then he shook his head. "How many men are still out looking for the Indian? I never thought the day would come when any of you would let a boss you don't like send you off on some wild-goose chase."

"No one sent us," one man replied. "This boss, he wasn't one bit pleased that anyone went."

"So what's going on, then?" Grandpa asked.

There was some shuffling. Looks passed from one man to another. Finally Cookee spoke up. "Something might've happened to Muskrat Mac. If he's all right, if there's no sign of him, then he's probably taken off. We just want to know for sure."

"What's going on is this," another man said. "If the boss doesn't care about one of us, he's not likely to care about the next. He doesn't match the man to the job. He just put a young woodsman with no river experience on the log drive. Then he tried to send the Indian out alone to clear a backlog. Only the Indian knows better. It won't take many more wrongheaded jobs before others, not just the Indian, will be moving on. We'll all be looking for work somewhere else."

As the tintypes went the rounds, Jonathan sized up the tiny portraits and compared them with the living faces. Much later, when he tried to recall what the men had been saying, he was astonished at what he had ignored. It wasn't as though he'd known he should be on the lookout for clues. After all, it was the end of a long, eventful day, and he was looking forward to dinner. With some men out looking for the Indian, there would be more fried fish for everyone here in camp.

Besides, there was no reason to suspect that this day had been any more eventful than it appeared.

ferent light, still absent in a way, perhaps in that foolish way Mama had warned about. Still, in another sense Grandpa seemed intensely present, as if he himself had become a camera, seeing, focusing, recording.

Even so, few sightings prompted a sudden halt and the lugging out of tripod and camera and glass. To break the monotony, Jonathan tried to predict which scene would prove to be the next irresistible lure. He usually picked sweeping views and dramatic skies. But Grandpa almost always confounded him, photographing instead the scaly lichen on a silver tree stump or a distant house at the edge of a planted field.

Often it wasn't until dark that Grandpa became fully attentive to ordinary matters, first seeing to Teddy, then making sure that Jonathan had something to eat before they crawled into the wagon and rolled themselves in their blankets for the night.

Except for one stop at a village store and another at a blacksmith, they went for days without speaking to another person. Finally they came to a farm where they were made welcome. There was a new baby in the house, and the parents wanted a photograph of the entire family.

For the family portrait every living thing on the farm was gathered into the front yard: hens and cats, a dog, a team of oxen, a mare soon to foal, as well as three older children and a granny. Few of these understood that while they posed before the camera, the slightest movement would produce a blurred image. Grandpa had to use up three precious glass plates, but he stayed calm and unhurried. After all, he had been invited to let Teddy out to pasture, and now there was the prospect of dinner in the farm kitchen.

11

Teddy was already harnessed and hitched to the wagon when Grandpa woke Jonathan. No one else was up but Cookee, who thrust a mug of sweet tea into Jonathan's hands and made sure he drank it right down. "You never know," Cookee said to him, and Jonathan understood that Cookee was speaking to Grandpa as well, urging him to give some thought to a growing boy's appetite.

"Don't worry," Grandpa responded.

Jonathan thanked Cookee with a sleepy grin.

On the long road there were long bouts of silence. Jonathan thought back to times like this when Grandpa, immersed in photography, seemed withdrawn from everyone and everything on the farm. Not much had registered before except Mama's silent disapproval. Dad usually shrugged off Grandpa's distancing, calling it one of his spells.

Jonathan had never thought much about it or wondered what it meant.

Now, though, he was beginning to see Grandpa in a dif-

As the day wore on, Grandpa kept on taking pictures, first in the house and later in the barn. He let Jonathan drag the tripod around and hand him glass plates.

"This needs longer exposure," he remembered to explain as he adjusted the big camera. "The less light, the more time."

While Grandpa prepared the family portrait, he developed the other pictures as well. He said he wanted to be sure before he left that he had caught the images he cared about. But he didn't touch any of the previously exposed plates, the ones of the river and loggers that he planned to develop later.

The brief spell on the farm was a relief for Jonathan. In the evening he went strawberry picking with the other children and regaled them with stories from his favorite dime novels. When they interrupted him to ask what a bootblack was, or a newsboy or a bank teller, he couldn't be bothered to explain. All he cared about was having listeners, even bewildered ones. An audience kept him sharp, so that words like "hoodlum" and "fervent" and "dastardly" came pouring out of him.

What the children made of this he couldn't tell. As soon as he finished, they began questioning him about his journey. They seemed more interested in the barn roof floating down the river than in tales of villainy on city streets, and they were deeply disappointed when he couldn't tell them where the rooster had ended up.

It wasn't until the next morning, after the extra pictures had been printed on specially coated paper, that Jonathan was able to see what had caught Grandpa's eye. Not anything Jonathan would have glanced at a second time, yet arresting once captured and fixed. Here the sun slanted through the barn door, light drenching a harness that hung on a post. The picture was mostly black, with only the hint of the interior wall and the bare outline of leather and shining buckles. And there was the granny seated by the root cellar, scrubbing carrots, her face all but lost in shadow, yet with the hairs escaping from beneath her cap as distinct and fine as a spider's web.

Once he and Grandpa were on the road again, it occurred to Jonathan that he should have paid attention to the developing and printing. Not that Grandpa seemed to care. He had been paid something more than hospitality for the family portrait, and he had photographs that satisfied him. These put him in a cheerful frame of mind.

12

After weeks of travel Grandpa was suddenly in a hurry. Even so, he paused above Masham to show Jonathan the whole of the town. Below them the river vanished behind immense stacks of logs and lumber and long sheds and the mill itself, a hulk at the bottom of the hill, dark and squat except for one tall stack.

Rising on the far side of the river, buildings of brick and wood fronted the main road, which forked, its two extensions skirting an open green before a steeper climb uphill. It was the mill, though, that dominated the town, the tall, smoking stack dwarfing even the church steeple at the head of the green.

"From here," said Grandpa, "you can tell where people fit. The meanest housing is down behind the carriage works and warehouses. That's for the millworkers. Their day starts at half past four in the morning and goes until seven in the evening. The foremen and overseers live farther up. See those square houses with porches? Most of the shop owners' homes are on that level, too, or just above. At the top, where there's part of a roof with turrets showing, that's where you'll find the millowner, Edwin Firth, who also owns a sizable portion of woodland up north."

Jonathan, who had seen pictures of castles with turrets in his schoolbook, thought the millowner must be someone very grand. "Do you know him?" he asked.

"I've done his portrait," Grandpa said dryly. "If Masham had a king, he'd be it."

They went on, downhill and over a bridge beside a dam that spanned the river. The waterfall beyond it produced a tidy spread of foam that seemed a far cry from the crashing rapids up north. Yet Jonathan could almost feel its power.

Progress through town was slow and noisy. Jonathan had never seen so many people in one place. Some, like a man selling whips beside the water trough, did business out-doors. Wagons and carriages and buggies standing at odd angles squeezed out others that could barely edge around them. Someone called out to Grandpa. Another person waved. Grandpa nodded right and left.

Jonathan gaped. There seemed to be a shop for everything in the world: drugs and confections, fishing tackle and ammunition, boots and shoes, groceries, lumbermen's sup-plies, barber, crockery and glassware, post office, livery sta-ble and blacksmith, inn and tavern (dining for ladies and gents), law offices, printers and signmaker, wilderness out-fitters, photograph gallery—

"Photograph gallery!" Jonathan exclaimed. "There's a photographer here."

"He's seasonal," Grandpa told him. "Everyone in town knows that." He grinned. "About to reopen."

Grandpa's gallery? Grandpa with a business of his own!

Did anyone in the family know this? Where did Grandpa fit on the hill?

Jonathan twisted around, trying not to miss anything. Suddenly he caught sight of a girl on a bicycle. He couldn't take his eyes off that. The girl wove in and out of obstacles with apparent ease, rising to pedal hard as the road began to ascend.

"Annie!" Grandpa called, drawing abreast of her.

The girl stopped, one booted foot on the road. "Uncle Rodney!" she exclaimed. "Ma's been waiting on you."

Uncle Rodney?

"I'm a mite late, I know," Grandpa said. "Want a lift up the hill? I can put your bicycle in the wagon."

The girl shook her head. "I'll go ahead of you. I'll tell Ma."

But she had to struggle to get the wheels to turn, and the bicycle wobbled back and forth before gaining enough momentum to take her farther.

"A mind of her own, like her mother," Grandpa muttered. He slowed Teddy so the girl could stay ahead of him, even when she had to walk her bicycle part of the way. Once she turned onto a side road that leveled off, she waved to him and went speeding out of sight.

"Are you her uncle?" Jonathan asked.

Grandpa shook his head. "It's what she calls me."

Jonathan was still mulling this when Grandpa halted Teddy in front of a gray house with attached sheds and a small barn. "Here we are," Grandpa announced as he rose stiffly and eased himself to the ground. The front door opened; out came the girl and Mrs. Noone.

"We almost gave up on you," Mrs. Noone scolded. But

she was smiling at him Then she looked up and saw Jonathan seated on the wagon. "Hello again, young man," she said. "What a surprise!"

Jonathan mumbled a greeting. He could feel the girl sizing him up—or down. His face went hot. He couldn't look back at her.

"Won't you join us?" Mrs. Noone said to him.

He jumped down from the wagon.

"You must become friends," she declared after she had introduced him to her daughter, Annie. Then, dropping her voice but still audible, she spoke to Grandpa. "What do we have here, Rodney?"

"What? Jonathan?" Grandpa shrugged. "He's supposed to learn photography."

"What is he really for?" she asked.

Grandpa cast her a brief glance that made her smile.

"Poor boy," she declared. "That's some assignment, becoming your errant grandfather's personal protector."

Jonathan felt the heat surge into his face again. It was unsettling to find that all along Grandpa had understood why he was saddled with his grandson. Probably a sharp detective like Wizard Will would have had it figured out from the start.

To escape Mrs. Noone's amused regard, Jonathan turned to Annie, who was scowling. He guessed she was trying to make sense of what had just been said.

Without her bicycle she looked quite ordinary, especially beside her well-dressed mother. In spite of the ribbon that tied back Annie's hair, dark strands fell about her smudged face. There was a small tear in the white pinafore she wore over her plain skirt and blouse, and her patched stockings and scuffed boots confirmed her disregard for herself. Still, she owned a bicycle. So in spite of her shabby appearance, that alone made her richer than anyone else he had ever known.

Annie helped unhitch Teddy and showed Jonathan where to take him. Mrs. Noone's horse stomped impatiently.

"That's enough of that, Ruby," Annie told it. "Hold your people."

"People?" said Jonathan.

"Well," Annie told him as she dropped hay into the stalls for both animals, "you can't expect a horse to hold its horses, can you?"

Unable to come up with a snappy answer, he dipped a rag in a tub of water and set to work scrubbing the sweat marks from Teddy's bay coat.

13

There were two Mrs. Noones in the gray house on Orchard Road. The second one was an Indian woman with bright-dark eyes and almost no teeth. Jonathan took her to be a hired hand until they were introduced. Then Grandpa added to Jonathan's confusion by addressing her as Grandmother.

After Grandpa explained that "Grandmother" was an Indian term of respect for elders, Jonathan thought he was beginning to understand, until Annie informed him that the woman really was her grandmother.

"She comes to us every winter," Annie explained as she led him through the shed and up the steep stairway to the wood-house chamber. "She doesn't talk much, but she has strong opinions. Even though she favors your grandfather, she still won't let him photograph her. But you'll find he can make her laugh." Annie was carrying a heavy pitcher of water, which she refused to hand over to Jonathan. "Granny wants me to learn the ways of my father's people."

"Your father was an Indian?" Jonathan exclaimed.

Annie shook her head. "Partly. Which makes me neither one thing nor the other. Granny hopes that if she can teach me to weave strong baskets and make fine thread from bark, I won't disgrace her. Since my mother's family disowned her when she married my father, I don't have to worry about disgracing them. Ma simply hopes I'll rise above all the adversity."

"Adversity?" Jonathan repeated. He was thinking that any girl who owned a bicycle and lived in a house with so many rooms that one could be kept ready for a seasonal lodger couldn't have much adversity to overcome.

"Like being called a half-breed," she said. "That's an adversity, and it's what people in Mr. Charles Dickens's novels rise above. Ma makes me read Dickens to inspire me."

"I read novels, too," Jonathan said.

"Oh, good," Annie declared, backing through the door into the wood-house chamber. "Maybe when you unpack your books we can exchange our favorites. Right now I'm halfway through *A Tale of Two Cities*. Have you read it?"

That name seemed to ring a bell, but Jonathan had to search his memory to extract the whole long title. Small wonder it took a moment to recall *Brooklyn Ben, the On-His-Own-Hook Detective, or Ned Chester's Very Bad Case: A Tale of Two Cities*. He said, "Yes, I read it last winter." He didn't admit that he hadn't realized it was by Charles Dickens.

"Don't tell me how it ends," Annie ordered. "I expect it will be sad. I love sad endings, don't you?"

Jonathan didn't know how to answer. Sad or happy didn't enter into his reckoning. "A story should come out right," he finally offered, meaning that the puzzle should be solved. "Justice . . ." He faltered. He wanted to say that justice must be done, but he was out of his depth with this girl and her powerful opinions. He was relieved when she deposited the pitcher beside the basin next to Grandpa's narrow bed and ran back downstairs to join the others.

The wood-house chamber, once used as the hired man's room, was spare but light, with a window overlooking a small fenced orchard behind the house. Jonathan would have to sleep on a mattress, which Annie's mother promised to provide.

But first she heated up water for a bath. Jonathan was mortified at having to strip down in a strange kitchen. While Grandpa seemed perfectly at home, Jonathan could feel the nearness of the two Mrs. Noones. And of Annie.

Even though he and Grandpa were more presentable for the evening meal, Jonathan was keenly aware of how wrinkled their clean clothes looked after several weeks rolled in a pack. But no one else at the table seemed to care.

Annie's mother's mind was on an important matter to do with something Grandpa had to prepare lest he miss a deadline. He didn't appear to consider it all that vital, though. Sounding slightly apologetic but also dismissive, he urged her not to fret. If he had missed this year's deadline, there was always next year. But Mrs. Noone insisted that he set aside everything else until he attended to what was needed.

Since Jonathan had no idea what they were talking about, he concentrated on the food, which included a new treat, tinned peaches. After dinner Mrs. Noone pored over some of Grandpa's photographs, setting aside those that were flawed.

"You'll make new prints at once," she told him.

"When I have time," he replied.

She rose and stood over him. "Rodney Capewell, it's now or never. You always let things go. There are cases of glass slides out in the shed from last fall. They're still waiting to be developed."

"If it's to be done to my own satisfaction," he said with surprising firmness, "I'll need to clear a space I don't yet have. And I will need to be left in peace."

Jonathan caught his breath. He wondered whether Mrs. Noone would be so offended that she would send them away. He studied the opposite end of the parlor with its small, draped tables adorned with decorative boxes and figurines and a lamp with a beaded fringe.

Annie sidled up to him and asked if he wanted to try riding her bicycle. But her mother overheard and said that must be put off. She didn't sound angry, but there was a crispness to her tone as she reminded Jonathan that he had not finished unpacking. As for Annie, surely there was a lesson due for school tomorrow.

Departing from the room, the two of them faced each other.

"What lesson?" Jonathan asked with a twinge of envy.

"Sums," Annie replied with a sigh. "Are you a good scholar for sums?"

"I suppose. Maybe I can do some with you?"

"Not some," she retorted. "Sums." She grinned at him.

"I mean, to help."

"Are you always so serious?" she said. "Anyway," she continued, "Ma wants you unpacking and me applying myself. Even when she's agitated like this, especially when she's busy with Uncle Rodney, she seems to have eyes in the back of her head."

Jonathan paused in the doorway. "I didn't know Grandpa had a deadline."

"I think it's a secret," Annie told him, her voice dropping. "Ma's been anxious for days. All I know is that it's about Uncle Rodney's pictures. It usually is. But since we're almost at the end of May, I expect it's also about Decoration Day, which he nearly missed. It's an important day here in Masham, but not nearly so much fun as July Fourth. I just don't know exactly what Ma has in mind. Sometimes she doesn't tell me things, so I have to puzzle them out for myself. I'm not one to wait and see."

Jonathan thought that was an understatement, but he kept his mouth shut. He went about carrying cases and glass holders up the steep stairs until it was too dark to see where he was going.

When Grandpa came up to the chamber to go to bed, he nearly tripped over some of the things that Jonathan had unloaded. "These don't belong here," he said, shaking his head. "I should have been showing you where to put the exposed plates instead of squandering the last of the daylight on Miranda's scheme."

Jonathan waited for some further explanation, but none came. By now he was too tired to care about much of anything, except the prospect of visiting the privy in the shed beyond the kitchen. If he found it being used, should he climb all the way back up the steep, dark stairs or just wait? He would never get used to this arrangement.

When finally, without a candle, he groped his way down and found the shed and privy empty, he decided it was a lucky sign. He needed something like this for his first night in Masham. Hold on to that luck, he told himself.

Just before he fell asleep, his thoughts wandered back to Annie. Even if her mother relented, he doubted he could ever be much help to anyone so sharp and stinging. He didn't know what to make of jokes like barbs aimed at puncturing his dullness. Her cleverness had tied his tongue; he hadn't been able to think of a single retort.

But now, as he lay in the dark, a few clever words began to gather in his head. If his luck held, they might yet take shape. In control at last, he would speak out, but with restraint, like Fergus Fearnaught putting a street tough in his place.

And if a street tough, why not Annie Noone?

14

During the first days in Masham there was so much to absorb that at times Jonathan felt like the rooster stranded on the raging river. Annie was in school, and Mrs. Noone seemed as busy as Grandpa, who never explained his living and working arrangement. Jonathan had to piece together scraps of information that came his way. No sooner was he accustomed to thinking of the photograph gallery above J & J Outfitters as Grandpa's studio than he had to adjust that assumption. It seemed that the gallery was somehow attached to J & J Outfitters, where Mrs. Noone worked. He still had no idea how the two businesses connected.

So many customers flocked to the photograph gallery that Grandpa never had a chance to sort out the things Jonathan had unloaded when they first arrived. Some of the glass plates he had brought to the wood-house chamber got shoved against the wall, and others were stacked with holders already stored in the downstairs shed.

For a while Grandpa attempted to store the newer plates according to a plan he never quite explained. He identified two containers of discards and one with plates he planned to work on as soon as possible. These got as far as the wagon, where they were shelved with those Jonathan hadn't removed that first evening. There they remained for the time being.

After Jonathan had learned how to wash glass plates so they could be used again, he offered to take care of the discards. But Grandpa didn't want to risk another mixup. He said he would get around to them before long.

Usually the moment Mrs. Noone suspected that Jonathan had nothing to do up in the gallery, she set him running errands for J & J Outfitters until it was time to go home. But with the end of May before them and Decoration Day's solemn celebration looming, there were additional glass plates to deal with and more orders for prints. So Grandpa kept Jonathan busy.

First thing on Decoration Day morning Grandpa made Jonathan go down into town to get ready. They were so early that the street was still being dragged to clean off horse droppings and to pack down the mud. Grandpa took a picture of the three horses hitched to the huge log that scraped the parade route and piled up a mound of refuse to be hauled away.

The holiday should have been a rare opportunity for Jonathan to explore the town. But as people gathered for the parade, Grandpa wandered off with the small box camera, leaving Jonathan to guard the big one he called The Monster.

When Annie pedaled by on her bicycle and offered to give him a lesson on it, he almost gave in to temptation. He couldn't imagine any harm coming to the big camera, which everyone in town knew. But he could imagine considerable harm coming to himself if he ran into Grandpa. So he remained stuck beside the tripod and camera and sent Annie on her way.

Up until now he had envied her being in school. But when he had to stand on a street corner and put up with boys and girls daring him to take pictures of them, he was grateful that tomorrow those children would be back inside the solid brick schoolhouse at the upper end of town.

Still, he wished he *could* take a picture. He would turn the camera toward the river and photograph, not the mill, silent for once, but the flags and bunting that framed the narrow way to and over the bridge. The water mirrored the dim light that escaped the low cloud cover. It was the only sliver of brightness on this dreary morning.

All day long people had been telling one another how fortunate it was that yesterday's rain had stopped in time for the parade and speechmaking. While the Civil War veterans assembled and band members rushed to take their places, a man paused to examine the camera. Jonathan stood as close as he could to show that the camera was not unattended. Finally the man asked Jonathan if it belonged to a gentleman by the name of— Here he faltered, trying to recall the name. So Jonathan supplied it.

"Rodney Capewell! Yes, that one. Is he about?"

Jonathan expected the man to move on when he learned that Mr. Capewell would probably be occupied all day. But the man took his time, examining the big camera and expressing surprise that such an unwieldy-looking device was still in use.

So Jonathan explained about different cameras for different purposes. Right now his grandfather was shooting photographs that could be printed as postcards or cabinet cards. This large camera was used for group pictures and outdoor scenes.

Since the man indicated that he was especially interested in the kinds of photographs it could make, Jonathan, aware that he was showing off, produced a spate of information about it, a good deal more than he'd realized he possessed. The man listened for a bit, then appeared to grow restless. Saying he looked forward to meeting Mr. Capewell, he walked away.

Jonathan almost forgot about him. There was so much to look at and listen to. The band played as if each musician wanted to be the loudest. To Jonathan it was thunderous and splendid. But when the band ceased playing and the former Union soldiers marched in step to a single drumbeat, he experienced a different kind of thrill. All the men lining the parade route removed their hats. Jonathan was so enthralled he just stood there. Then he felt his cap lifted from his head. He thought Grandpa had returned, but to his shame it was the stranger who handed him the cap.

It was hard to look up at him. But instead of finding a rebuke in the stranger's gaze, he saw only blandness like a mask across his eyes.

After the old soldiers had marched by and the band resumed playing, the man brushed off Jonathan's apology. "I'd guess this is your first parade," he remarked.

Jonathan said it was, that he was new in town. When the stranger asked him where he was from, Jonathan told him about home and about his travels. Out of nervousness or relief, he kept on talking until the man took his leave once more.

Jonathan figured he'd driven the stranger away again, but later, when the sun burned through the cloud cover and began to steam up the town, the man returned with an open bottle of sarsaparilla for Jonathan.

Just then Grandpa appeared. It was time to carry the tripod and camera and plates up to the town green for the speeches. Jonathan didn't know what to do about the sarsaparilla. Would Grandpa pay for it? The stranger, who said he had been waiting to meet Mr. Capewell, offered to help carry the equipment. Grandpa only half listened as he hoisted up the heavy camera and the container of glass plates. The man took up the tripod and fell into step beside him.

Jonathan carried the box camera in one hand and the sarsaparilla in the other. Walking behind the two men, he heard the stranger invite Grandpa to call him Fred. Since Grandpa appeared to be warming to his helpful new acquaintance, Jonathan decided it was all right to accept the refreshment. But he kept out of their sight as he raised the bottle and took one delicious sip after another.

Later, under the sun's glare, Fred removed his hat to mop his sweaty forehead, and Jonathan was struck by an oddity he had noticed earlier during the solemn moment in the parade when Fred had stood hatless in the morning haze. At the time Jonathan had been consumed by his own embarrassment and hadn't given the man's appearance more than a passing thought.

But now he could see that Fred really did seem to own two faces, the upper one tanned and weathered, the lower one pale and slightly drawn. This impression of the attentive stranger had sent an image skipping across Jonathan's mind. It came to him again: mask.

As soon as he had identified the image, he was able to let it go. There was still a chance he might get away while there was time for a bicycle lesson. He would find Annie and leave the affable Fred to Grandpa.

15

As soon as school let out for the summer, Annie was put to work helping Ernie, Mrs. Noone's assistant, at J & J Outfitters. But it wasn't long before Annie began to take over some of Jonathan's errands for the gallery. That made Grandpa scowl at Jonathan and complain how slow he was.

When Jonathan saw her return on her bicycle after making a delivery for Grandpa, he met her at the store entrance and complained that she was getting him in trouble. She flared up at him. "Trade places, then," she said. "I'll work for Uncle Rodney, and you work for Ma."

He almost wished they could switch. While she went cycling around town, he was stuck inside setting up a flight balloon prop for a portrait session with two young girls. Grandpa, who disliked this kind of photography, had just escorted them and their mother up to the studio, where the girls were supposed to wave cheerfully from the cardboard gondola.

"Take a stand," Annie ordered. "Yes or no."

Annie might be able to persuade two shy children to look

as though they couldn't wait to go soaring into the sky. But Grandpa had just lectured Jonathan about shirking his responsibilities, so he said nothing.

Annie added on a frantic note, "Don't you care what you do?"

Jonathan said, "I'm supposed to learn photography."

"And I'm supposed to learn basketmaking. And how to run Ma's business. But I don't want to do what she does. Besides, she learned from my father, and I suppose he learned from his father, who started the business after he'd been a woodland guide."

"It's a good living, isn't it?" Jonathan asked, registering the fact that Mrs. Noone owned it.

Annie shrugged. "It's good in the summer, slow in winter, and it's dull all year round. I'd rather study photography. Last year Uncle Rodney said he'd teach me, too. Then you came. Anyway, if you won't trade work with me, I'll go with Grandmother to her Indian relations. At least it'll be a change."

Jonathan said, "Really? Can you do that?" He almost asked if he could use her bicycle while she was gone.

But she took his response as a challenge. "Just you wait and see!" she declared, flinging herself away from him.

As Jonathan suspected, the children appeared terrified of Grandpa and his camera. Their mother's command to smile only pasted grimaces on their tense little faces. At least the rigid expressions matched the starched dresses. Except for the limp handkerchief that was supposed to be waved, everything was as stiff as the cardboard prop.

Grandpa could barely contain his irritation. Behind the camera Jonathan clowned for all he was worth, but to no avail. Disgusted, he ducked his head in the crook of his arm, stamped his foot, and made a show of crying his eyes out. Sneaking a glance, he saw he had at last caught the girls' attention. So he kept up this act until the light flashed and a puff of smoke signaled the finish of the picture. From the studio doorway someone clapped.

The someone turned out to be Fred, the Decoration Day stranger. After the customer and her children had departed, Grandpa asked in a frosty tone if the man wished to make an appointment.

Fred met this rebuff with almost strident cheerfulness. "I stopped by to see how you are doing and in hope that you have the pictures we spoke of."

"Mr. Whittaker," Grandpa said, "those plates aren't even developed. At this time of year I have all I can do to keep up with paying orders."

"If any of those river pictures suit me, you may charge me a hefty price," the man said. "And call me Fred."

"Fred, then," Grandpa replied. "If you're in a hurry for river pictures, you'd better look elsewhere. There are photographers in Bangor who may have some on hand."

"But yours will be up-to-date. Look, Rodney, why don't you let me take care of the printing? I could bring the plates to Bangor."

Grandpa shook his head. "That's my real photography. I won't know what I have until I work with those negatives."

"Of course," Fred Whittaker replied. "I understand. I understood on Decoration Day. Anyone who chooses to take pictures rather than to march with fellow heroes of the Union army is a man who is dedicated to his profession."

"Then you'll understand that I must get on with it," Grandpa declared, turning in to the darkroom and shutting the door behind him.

Fred Whittaker smiled at Jonathan. "That was a fine performance, my boy. You really helped your grandfather."

Grandpa's rudeness left Jonathan feeling awkward. "I have to go. To fetch water," he explained as he grabbed two empty buckets and hurried down the outside stairs. "The prints take a lot of rinsing."

Mr. Whittaker followed him to the pump. "These look heavy," he said "Let me help." Before Jonathan could object, the man had one full bucket and was on his way upstairs with it.

"Don't open the door," Jonathan warned as Fred Whittaker approached the darkroom.

"No, of course not. I'm aware that pictures can be spoiled. Do you know there's a new camera now that uses rolled film and takes many pictures at once? The film is developed at the camera factory. People say the new system will put photographers like your grandfather out of business."

Jonathan, who had already heard about the new type of camera, suddenly recalled Fred Whittaker's interest in the old monster camera. "Grandpa thinks the new kind won't be as good for his kind of photography," said Jonathan, holding the door to the outside stairs so that Mr. Whittaker could precede him.

"You mean like the kind I'm trying to get hold of?" said Mr. Whittaker. "I suppose he may be right. Come to think of it, maybe you know where those glass plates are. It would save him a deal of time."

"They could be anywhere," Jonathan explained, hoping he sounded apologetic. "Maybe even in the wagon. But I'm not allowed to touch exposed plates."

Mr. Whittaker said, "A safe rule, I'm sure. I'm just chafing to get hold of them for advertising, and I can't wait forever."

Trying to sound agreeable, Jonathan expressed his own eagerness to see the pictures. "There was a roof on the river," he added. "An oddity. No one's ever seen the like of it."

"A picture of that sort would catch people's attention. Although," Mr. Whittaker said, "the logging and river drives should be the principal attraction." Noting Jonathan's puzzlement, Mr. Whittaker added, "Your grandfather didn't tell you that I intend to run wilderness tours up north?"

Jonathan shook his head. He wasn't about to inform Mr. Whittaker that from Decoration Day until now Grandpa had not once mentioned his name.

16

Walking up the hill at the end of the day, Annie's mother spoke to no one. It was the first time Jonathan had seen her lose her composure. He guessed this was a reaction to Annie's proposal—or threat.

But when he dropped behind to ask Annie about it, she said she hadn't even mentioned her new plan. Her mother's bad mood had something to do with Granny. "Only Ma isn't talking about it yet. All I know is I missed a deal of excitement."

This was one of the days Grandmother helped out in the store. As usual, she had brought baskets to sell to tourists stopping off on their journey to the new hotel on the lake. Since many of them had come straight from the train to the stage, they were glad to get out and stretch their legs when the stage stopped for refreshment at the Masham Inn. Those who found their way into J & J Outfitters were often eager to acquire real Indian basketry.

So what could have happened to Grandmother? As far as Jonathan could tell, she looked the same as she had this morning, except that her homecoming load of baskets was smaller.

Annie said, "Could I take one of your dime novels with me when I go? I'll let you borrow my books."

Even though he knew both detective stories practically by heart, he hated to give one up. Still, since Annie had given him bicycle lessons, he couldn't possibly refuse her. So he nodded. "I've said all along you can have them right here."

"But Ma thinks they're unsuitable for me. You know that. Please, Jonathan, just one. I won't lose it."

"You don't even know if you're really going," he reminded her. In any event, lacking new dime novels, he would soon have to resort to some of her thick books.

She squared her shoulders and said, "I'll know soon enough. As soon as the uproar over Granny dies down. I'm just waiting for Ma to, well, speak."

"To speak about your grandmother?"

Annie cast him a withering look. "No. Don't you understand? To speak about any ordinary thing. Then I'll know she's recovered from whatever happened."

At the house everyone attended to chores. The two Mrs. Noones fixed supper without, it seemed, exchanging a word. Grandpa, who refused to pay anyone to do what he could do for himself, went to work resoling his boots. Jonathan watered and fed the horses in the orchard. Afterward, passing the open door to the second shed, he came across Annie sorting basket materials.

"This brown ash," she said, "gets all jumbled up with the maple, which is only used for hoops and bales." Her neutral tone made him think that she was distancing herself from her earlier mood. He felt strangely relieved.

They all were seated around the table when Annie announced her intention.

At first, taken by surprise, Jonathan didn't know where to look. It had never occurred to him that her apparent retreat had been a girding up for conflict.

To his amazement Annie's mother calmly answered, "If Grandmother has no objection, you may prepare some clothes. You needn't make a final decision about spending the summer with her until she is with her relatives. But," Mrs. Noone added, "you will stick to that decision once it's made. That will mean staying with Grandmother until the fall, when I fetch you both home."

No one spoke. Grandmother could be heard sucking marrow from a cracked bone. Jonathan glanced at Annie, who had gone pale, but only for an instant. Now a red spot stained each of her cheeks and slowly spread over her face. Her eyes were very dark, very bright. For the first time Jonathan detected the trace of a likeness between her and her grandmother.

Finally Grandpa said conversationally, "Maybe while you're away, we'll clean out the shed. Fix a place for Jonathan to start some photography on his own."

"An excellent idea, Rodney," Mrs. Noone responded. "I suspect you'll find a good supply of silver nitrate and that emulsion you said may be running short. With your things spread over three different places, we need a proper inventory before placing the next order."

Grandmother mumbled something more, and Annie's

mother said quickly, "No, no, not your space. Rodney wouldn't touch your things."

"Now, Grandmother," Grandpa said to the old woman, "you know I never interfere."

Annie's mother said that Grandmother was on edge because someone with a camera had tried to take her picture outside the store.

"A photographer?" Grandpa exclaimed.

"One of the tourists off the stage. They go about town with those wooden box cameras. They're the latest thing."

"So after all my self-restraint," Grandpa said to the older Mrs. Noone, "you let an ignorant outsider come along and snap you with a newfangled shadow-catcher?"

"Don't tease," Annie's mother told him. "To Grandmother it's an affront."

"Of course it is," Grandpa said. "Even if she is the last of her people to object to picture taking."

"She did more than object," Annie's mother told him.

"What did you do, Grandmother?" he inquired.

"Shadow-catcher," the older Mrs. Noone replied. "Bust him."

"You broke a camera?" Annie exclaimed. "Right there on the street?"

"She tried." Annie's mother sighed. "There was quite a set-to out there. The tourist wanted to press charges, but he couldn't without staying behind when the stage left. I promised Constable Stebbins that Grandmother wouldn't assault anyone again."

Grandpa's mouth twitched as if it wanted to break into a smile. "Well done," he declared. Jonathan couldn't tell which Mrs. Noone he was addressing.

Annie's mother fixed him with her steady gaze. "I also promised Grandmother that if another tourist with a camera attempts such a trick, you'll bust it for her."

Grandpa bowed to Grandmother. "Just call on me," he said. "I'd be proud to serve."

Grandmother nodded with satisfaction and left the table.

Grandpa and the younger Mrs. Noone exchanged a look. "A taxing day," he commented. "Taxing all around." At last the smile came and held between them.

Annie said, "Don't you even care that I may be gone all summer? Haven't you anything else to say about it?"

The others turned to her.

Mrs. Noone was the first to reply. "My dear child," she said, "I care that you want to go."

Grandpa remarked, "I suppose there will be tourists wherever your grandmother may be. I trust we can count on you to stand in as resident camera buster."

Before Jonathan could summon the courage to ask Annie what she intended to do with the bicycle, she stormed into the kitchen, where she began pumping water furiously into the kettle. It sizzled as she slapped it down on the stove, but that was only a modest display compared with the clatter the dishpan made when she dropped it into the sink.

17

It took Annie a few days to come to terms with what she had set in motion. Since her mother had called her bluff, she became resigned to playing the role she had cast for herself. Putting resentment aside, she plunged into all those tasks from which she had so recently rebelled.

Jonathan considered this new cordial and agreeable Annie a vast improvement over the old one. All the same, he didn't quite trust the transformation.

She was especially agreeable when the trip to Grandmother's relatives was postponed, first because of torrential rain and after that because of its being too close to July Fourth. That was when Annie's mother would be selling the novelties she had been making all winter long.

The novelties were stored in the shed alongside some of Grandpa's glass negative plates. Annie lifted the dust cover from a basket to give Jonathan a glimpse of balsam pincushions with words like "Piety!" and "Industry!" stitched across the top in swirling letters. "Ma says these mostly serve local tastes," Annie told him. "A lot of tourists prefer the cushions that say, 'Souvenir of Masham.' "

She reached for a crate and nodded at the one beneath it for him to pick up. "Ma wants these in the parlor." After she set hers down, she raised its lid. Peering inside, Jonathan frowned in puzzlement.

"Bracelets," she declared, picking up a braided circlet. "See?"

"It looks like hair," he said.

"It is. These are very popular. Ma makes a few to order, but we sell most of them on the Fourth of July. Some people give us locks of their own hair to go with their portraits. That's where Uncle Rodney comes in. He takes the tintypes to slip into little cases that attach to the clasps. And these," she added, pointing to another tray of bracelets made of black hair, "are for mourning. Ma gets Indian hair from Granny's relatives."

Still puzzled, Jonathan said that at home no one sold anything on the Glorious Fourth. It was a patriotic day with a picnic and sometimes baseball, nothing more.

"What about fireworks?" Annie asked him

He shook his head. He had never seen fireworks.

Annie said, "I didn't think you lived that far away from civilization. People come from miles around to celebrate the Fourth here in Masham. There's an even bigger parade than on Decoration Day, and afterward races and games and baseball and then a huge outdoor chicken roast and finally the fireworks. And we make money."

Annie's mother sat beside her sewing table, opened a small box, and launched into a one-sided conversation. "We ran out of these clasps last winter. Then by the time the new order arrived, I was involved in another project. Have you seen the velvet photograph album covers? They're my crowning achievement. After those were finished, the store claimed all my attention, as it always does in the spring."

He nodded. He knew that was all the response she expected from him.

She smiled ruefully. "I try to keep up," she continued. "Not only to set an example for Annie, who might otherwise think all grown people, like your grandfather, get by putting things off. But," she finished with a sigh, "one can do only so much."

For a few minutes Jonathan watched with fascination as Annie and her mother attached delicate clasps to each length of intricately braided hair. It was hard to imagine Mrs. Noone spending an entire winter producing such curious adornments.

He had just about stopped comparing her household with the farm. At home kitchen ashes were always soaked in a trough to produce lye for soap. Here in Masham, where there wasn't a leaching trough in sight, cakes of soap came from the store along with all manner of food in tin cans. As for laundry, once a week a Mrs. Shriver appeared at the house to wash and iron. Also, while Mama constantly sewed to keep the family clothed, here Mrs. Noone ran a business in town and earned extra money embroidering velvet album covers and weaving bracelets out of human hair.

"Jonathan," Mrs. Noone said to him, "will you read aloud? Annie reads to me on winter evenings. It helps keep the mind occupied during tiresome tasks."

Caught idle, he had to oblige. "I might not read as well as Annie," he warned.

"It doesn't matter. It will be a change," Mrs. Noone told him. "Why don't you pick something you especially like?"

Annie jumped up. "I'll help choose," she said, leading the way to the bookcase. Standing beside him, she ran her fingers along the spines of the volumes. "Here," she declared, pulling out a book. "I finished this awhile back. And you already know it, so you'll be able to read with expression."

Glancing at the title she proffered, he saw that it was Dickens's *A Tale of Two Cities.* He didn't have to look inside to see that this was not last winter's dime novel. "You won't want to hear this so soon again," he protested, certain that as soon as he started in on this book, his mistake would be obvious.

"Yes, I will," she insisted. "It'll be different now that I know how it ends." She returned to her chair and picked up her work.

Jonathan had no choice but to open the book to the first page and begin reading, " 'It was the best of times, it was the worst of times, it was the age of wisdom, it was the age of foolishness. . . . ' " He had never known a story to begin this way. As the words drew him in, he forgot to worry that his ignorance would be exposed.

Grandpa joined them, an envelope of prints in hand. Even when Mrs. Noone set aside a bracelet to look at his photographs, even when she murmured comments over them, Jonathan read on. Already he knew better than to look for a Fergus Fearnaught or a Wizard Will to leap out of these pages, spinning toward the customary dime-novel climax in which justice is bound to prevail.

18

Just before the Fourth of July Grandpa showed Jonathan how to shoot and prepare tintypes. He even took time to introduce Jonathan to the cameras used for better pictures. But he also made Jonathan take charge of Teddy, and that included cleaning and polishing harness and setting the wagon to rights.

"The way it's arranged for the fairs," Grandpa explained unhelpfully.

Jonathan appealed to Annie, who told him that once the summer and fall fairs began, Uncle Rodney was on the road a great deal, and the wagon was turned into a full-fledged studio. "Otherwise," she went on, "if it rains, he loses all his business."

The interior of the wagon looked pretty much as it had when they first came to Masham. There was the frypan, still greasy from its last use, and here the potato barrel with tiny sprouts pressing through a crack. Some of those exposed glass plates remained, too, very likely including the ones Fred Whittaker had asked for.

Grandpa had intended to bring them to the gallery.

Should they be stacked together with others in the shed that he also meant to develop? Or did Grandpa plan to move them as soon as Teddy was hitched to the wagon again? If Grandpa wouldn't say what he wanted, how could Jonathan make it presentable enough to suit him?

"Start with a broom, rags, and a scrub brush," Annie suggested. "I'll get them. You do the water. We'll need buckets and buckets."

"I shouldn't let you help," Jonathan said without much conviction.

"You can help me next time I have a dreary task," she told him.

"Like what?" he said, suddenly wary.

Annie shrugged. "Airing mattresses. That's a dreadful chore."

Jonathan was about to protest that it was women's work, but something made him swallow that remark. "I guess that's fair," he mumbled.

And it was, he supposed, when he saw how Annie pitched in. By the end of the morning they both looked as though most of the accumulated filth of the wagon had been transferred to them.

When Grandpa and Mrs. Noone returned home at lunchtime, they exchanged one of their looks. Jonathan expected a blast for allowing Annie to help, but Grandpa merely regarded the debris stacked outside the wagon, peeked in, and nodded. Mrs. Noone inspected more thoroughly and remarked that it could do with a fresh coat of paint.

She wouldn't let either of them in the house. Instead they ate egg sandwiches, lemonade, and gingerbread in the cool barn. Afterward Mrs. Noone appeared with overalls and an oversize shirt. "These belonged to your father," she said to Annie. "Put them on over everything else and roll up the legs." She turned to Jonathan. "This shirt already has stains," she said, "but that's not a license to be sloppy. Besides, there's not much paint left in the can, so have a care with the brush."

They had to remove the trays and bottles and glass holders first. To their dismay there were more spots and rings in need of soap and water. Jonathan argued that the paint would cover those marks, but Annie snapped that she hadn't worked all morning to leave the job half done. She almost sounded like her old self.

Still, they managed to get through the afternoon without being in each other's way. When Annie found that no amount of turpentine would clean up the spatters and drip marks, it was Jonathan who solved the problem by painting the entire wagon floor. Even though it meant they couldn't finish the wheel rims, they did cover all the spokes.

The effect was interesting. That was what Grandpa said. But Mrs. Noone rummaged in the barn until she found a small can of black touch-up paint, enough for the wheel rims and the portable steps.

"Tomorrow," she said as Grandpa draped a canvas tarpaulin over the photograph equipment stacked on the grass. "Wash up now."

Grandpa said, "You'll need to give it another day to dry. Meanwhile we'll collect what we need to take from the gallery. And you'll practice with tintypes."

Annie and Jonathan basked in the unspoken approval of their elders, which took the form of freedom until dark.

They took turns running and riding the bicycle all the way down to the bridge. Jonathan had grown so used to the constant whine of the sawmill that the clear sound of many voices seemed almost unnatural.

There was a festive air to the groups clustered in front of the inn or strolling by. Jonathan and Annie lingered, listening and watching, not speaking.

They were standing on the bridge, looking down at boats from a river drive, when someone touched Jonathan's shoulder. He wheeled around to find Mr. Whittaker smiling at him.

"Fine evening," Mr. Whittaker said, tipping his hat to Annie. "How's your grandfather?" he asked Jonathan.

Jonathan thought it was extremely civil of the man to inquire after Grandpa after their last encounter. He said his grandfather was well.

"If I don't run into him in the next day or so, kindly tell him that I had no luck in Bangor, which, by the way, is mobbed with carousing rivermen. If he happens to have located those photographs, he can leave a message for me at the inn."

Jonathan suspected that the glass plates Mr. Whittaker had in mind were in one of the containers under the canvas waiting for the paint to dry. "I know he expects to develop some of his own pictures before the fair season begins," Jonathan said, not wanting to promise too much. "Probably those river pictures have been in the wagon all along. After the Fourth he means to bring them to the gallery to sort through them."

"Well, it's a pity I can't stay very long in town. Business calls me back to Bangor. But I thank you for your help."

"What help?" Annie said after Mr. Whittaker had left them. "You didn't help him."

"Well," Jonathan answered, "I tried to. Sort of."

Annie shook her head. "Why doesn't he go to Uncle Rodney?"

Jonathan said, "Grandpa was rude to him last time. I don't think he meant to be. He was just feeling pressed. Before that they'd been friendly. Then Mr. Whittaker showed up at the wrong time."

Annie scowled.

While it was obvious to Jonathan that she had taken against Mr. Whittaker, it wasn't at all clear why. Thinking she was often too quick to judge, Jonathan merely remarked that Mr. Whittaker had been helpful as well as interested in Grandpa's work.

But Annie shook her head, as if she didn't quite believe him. Her loosened hair revealed a patch of white.

Jonathan fell silent. He already knew that when she became notional like this, it was pointless to try to change her mind. He certainly had no intention of informing her of the swath of paint that streaked her dark brown hair.

They walked the bicycle home together, both of them suddenly feeling the effects of the long day's work.

19

It was still dark when Grandpa went out to feed Teddy. By the time the rest of the household was in the kitchen for breakfast, dawn was just breaking. Grandpa chivied everyone. If they hurried, he would be the first vendor in Firth Field, where most of the activities would take place. He wanted to secure his usual position near the big oak tree that would shade Teddy through the hottest time of day.

The two Mrs. Noones held firm against him. The day would be long, they said as they poured coffee and flipped pancakes and turned bacon. The children should start it with a nourishing meal.

Jonathan, who hadn't shaken the memory of those first hungry days on the road with Grandpa, ate as if to ward off starvation. But Annie was on Grandpa's side. Even though the wagon was already loaded up, she still had last-minute touches for the harness. She kept popping out of her chair, only to be ordered back to the table to finish what was on her plate.

"I can't," she protested. "I'll be ill."

"In that case you'd better stay home," her mother told her.

Annie mopped up maple syrup with the last forkful of pancake and stuffed it into her mouth.

Later, admiring Teddy, his black mane and forelock sporting red, white, and blue streamers, she said, "He belongs in the parade." But Jonathan's eyes were on all the decorations in town and then, after the steep drive uphill, on the imposing granite pillars and solid stone wall that marked the entrance to Mr. Firth's residence. Grandpa drove Teddy past that entrance and on along a cart track that led to the fenced field that Mr. Firth made available every July Fourth for the town's festivities.

Just inside the field Grandpa turned Teddy full circle and stopped with the wagon angled away from the wire fence. This created a protected area for selling baskets and novelties and for picture taking. The beribboned horse was tied to a weathered fence post near the tree that would shelter him from the afternoon sun.

Grandpa and the two Mrs. Noones, who stayed to set up the wagon studio and the sales booth, let Jonathan and Annie take off to scout out a spot for watching the parade. On the town green, the final loop of the parade route, they chose a tree with a low limb for a perch. The limb, which elbowed out and then up, allowed them to see over the heads of those who lined the street.

That started a trend. Pretty soon more boys and a few girls were using trees as perches, until a father called two girls down and scolded them for making an unladylike show of themselves. One of them defended herself by pointing to Annie, only to be told that such behavior could be expected from that sort of girl.

"What does he mean?" Jonathan asked Annie, who was staring straight ahead, her face expressionless.

"You know," Annie said.

"I don't," Jonathan insisted.

"He's talking about mixed breeding. As far as he reckons, I'm nothing. ·If he had his way, he'd split my last name in two and call me Annie No One."

"Noone to no one!" Jonathan exclaimed just as the band announced the start of the parade. "I never thought of that!"

"There's a lot you never think of," Annie muttered under cover of a rousing march.

Once again flag-bearing veterans led the ranks. Then came wagons carrying scenes with people posed in costumes and performers showing off special skills. Jonathan and Annie argued about which was best: a team of massive dapple gray horses pulling a bright red fire pump carriage with a big brass bell, or a hurdy-gurdy player with a monkey that picked up coins tossed to it. Then a tall juggler on stilts swaggered into view and won over both of them.

Every time the man on stilts paused to juggle yellow balls, he held up the parade behind him. Sometimes he threw a ball to one of the spectators. He seemed to know which person would lob it back to him so that he could continue his act. But once he had to call out sharply, "Heads up, mister!" to alert the catcher, and another time the ball fell, sending children scrambling for it. A clown on a great-wheeled bicycle intercepted one toss and refused to return it.

Jonathan stood up to follow the antics of the juggler and the clown. As the parade came around the far side of the green, the clown hurled the stolen ball at a man in the crowd. Someone shouted, "Heads up, mister!" But the man was caught off guard. He lurched and ducked and then, as if suddenly changing his mind, slammed the ball with all his might. A boy in a tree caught it and threw it properly to the juggler, who resumed his sport.

"That was your Mr. Whittaker," Annie remarked with a scowl.

Jonathan said, "Yes. It was." The fun had soured, and he didn't know why. It wasn't only that Annie was out of sorts. Mr. Whittaker's almost savage blow had sent a chill through him. He was seeing it in two places, two times. It was like one of Grandpa's rare mistakes, when one picture was shot on top of another. Here was Mr. Whittaker smashing the ball into the treetops, and there, almost in place, was the man in the checked shirt whacking at a desperate, flapping rooster.

"Let's go," Annie said.

"I'll race you to the field," he challenged, trying to bring back the fun.

But the crowds were too thick, and anyway, they were better off taking their time, because as soon as they reached the wagon, they both were put to work.

20

Jonathan was so busy that he missed most of the games and contests. Horseshoes were pitched all day, but the chopping and sawing competitions were limited. So were the children's games. Grandpa said Jonathan could run in the obstacle race, but when the time came, they both were taking pictures, and Jonathan lost his chance.

He had thought he was only going to develop the tintypes. But so many customers preferred bigger pictures that Grandpa was kept busy taking photographs for cabinet cards and had to hand over all the tintype production to his grandson.

At times Jonathan shouldered the camera and wandered around the vast field, offering tintypes wherever people gathered.

Whenever he returned to develop an exposed sheet in the wagon, Annie fixed him with an envious glare. She had to stand with the two Mrs. Noones behind boards spread across sawhorses. A tablecloth provided a clean counter on which to display the baskets and cushions and other souvenirs. After each set of tintypes was finished and cut, Annie came around to pick up the few that were to be inserted in bracelets. Otherwise she was stuck there showing and selling and making change.

Jonathan was out enjoying the milling crowds when he ran into Mr. Whittaker.

"So you've been promoted to assistant photographer," Mr. Whittaker declared. "Good for you. I'll mark the occasion with a picture."

"You're going to pose for a tintype?" Jonathan asked in surprise.

"I'll pay for one. What or who would you choose to take?"

That was easy, a gift for Annie. "The monkey," Jonathan said.

"Go ahead then," Mr. Whittaker told him, proffering the money.

Jonathan pulled back. He didn't feel right accepting this kind of gift.

Mr. Whittaker smiled. "Let it be a keepsake, to remember your first day behind the camera."

Gratitude tempered Jonathan's resistance and prompted him to mention that if the rush for pictures slowed, his grandfather might have a chance to find those glass plate negatives in the wagon. But Mr. Whittaker shook his head. "I've seen how busy he is. I won't trouble him today."

Jonathan put off returning to the studio wagon until he located the monkey. It was retrieving balls in a contest for young children, who were supposed to knock over a cutout wooden moose. As soon as parents noticed Jonathan and his camera, they lined up to get pictures of their little contestants. The hurdy-gurdy man didn't appreciate having his customers or his monkey distracted, so he charged Jonathan ten cents for the privilege of taking one picture.

Jonathan returned to the wagon with a pocketful of change, only not quite enough. He couldn't decide whether borrowing the missing ten cents from Annie, who usually had spending money, would be like making her pay for her gift.

As the day heated up, it got harder for Jonathan and Grandpa not to bump into each other or splash the developing and fixing compounds that made Jonathan's eyes tear. But by midafternoon the expected shade brought some relief. Grandpa lengthened Teddy's tether so he could graze but kept him hitched up. Then Annie's mother convinced Grandpa to take some time for himself, and he went with her to hear the band.

When they finally returned laden with iced cakes and lemonade, they were in high spirits. Mrs. Noone had talked Grandpa into staying for the fireworks.

Soon after, everyone caught the first whiff of potatoes and chicken beginning to sizzle over yards of stone-bound embers. When the pie wagon arrived, children ran alongside, trying to jump on it or stretch tall to peek at that rare vision, an entire cartload of desserts.

And still people came for pictures, sometimes posing with Teddy, sometimes using one of the cardboard props Grandpa had brought. Annie's mother eventually made a foray into the food area to bring supper to everyone, but they had to take turns eating the deliciously scorched dinner.

As the light began to fade and the band resumed playing,

people moved off to settle on blankets and await the fire-works. It was time to pack up, first the breakables, next the large equipment like the sawhorses and boards and props, and finally the few remaining items that hadn't sold.

The older Mrs. Noone was just starting down the hill when Grandpa picked up his moneybox and fell into step beside her.

"Rodney!" Annie's mother called to him. "You promised to stay." She turned to Jonathan. "Usually he leaves the wagon here for Annie and me and walks home with Grand-mother. But she's fine on her own, and this is your first fire-works."

Annie shouted, "Please, Uncle Rodney, just this once. It will be like a family party."

Jonathan was vaguely aware that this might be the kind of occasion his own family was counting on him to pre-vent. But he dismissed the thought, because he hadn't the slightest idea how to go about keeping Grandpa out of Mrs. Noone's clutches—if that was what this almost family party was about.

Grandpa gave in, and the four of them made their way onto the knoll, where the tablecloth that had covered the boards was spread on the grass. Mrs. Noone had also brought a "Souvenir of Masham" cushion, which she used to recline on, while Grandpa tried to fold his creaking legs first one way and then another. He kept shifting uncom-fortably, but he stayed beside Mrs. Noone, and they even sang together when the band played a song they both knew.

Jonathan felt in his pocket for the tintype of the little monkey. Maybe tomorrow he would give it to Annie when she awoke to an ordinary morning, or else the next day, when she set off with her mother and grandmother to visit the relatives.

The fireworks began before it was pitch dark. At the first bang Jonathan clapped his hands over his ears and pressed hard. But as the night sky went black and explosions splintered the horizon, he got used to the shrill, piercing whistles that preceded the deafening crashes.

"Roman candles!" Annie yelled in his ear. "They're even better than rockets."

He gazed awestruck at each display. The bombardment was almost continuous, with minor reports like gunshots coming, it seemed, from all around the field. His ears throbbed. A burning smell filled his nostrils. Overhead threads of smoke wrote magic script that swelled into sinuous clouds and vanished as it fell to earth.

In the midst of the show Grandpa struggled to his feet and whispered hoarsely that he would wait in the wagon.

Mrs. Noone got up at once, whipped the tablecloth over her arm, and ordered Annie and Jonathan to follow. When Annie started to object, her mother turned back and whispered sharply, "We're going with your uncle Rodney."

"But why?" Annie cried.

"Hush!" Mrs. Noone ordered. "It hurts his head. It brings the war back for him. I shouldn't have coaxed him to stay. I thought tonight might be different."

She went weaving around families and couples seated on the grass, all eyes on the brilliance in the sky. The explosions sounded so close, so violent, that for an instant Jonathan lost his bearings. Why couldn't he find the wagon?

In an interval of absolute darkness he stumbled into

Grandpa, which meant they both must have strayed from the correct course. Only wasn't that fence post just ahead of them the one where Teddy had been tied? Grandpa seemed to think so. At least he groped toward it.

The sky flared up again, and in the lurid flash Jonathan saw Grandpa holding a short length of Teddy's rope, still attached to the post.

21

"Don't worry," Mrs. Noone shouted after Grandpa, "Teddy knows his way home."

Grandpa kept on calling as he raced out of the field.

Annie said, "Teddy never runs away."

Her mother said, "Keep back. The last thing we need is either of you meeting up with an overexcited horse."

Along the cart track leading to the road Jonathan saw lanterns bobbing. People rushed toward Grandpa. First the lanterns surrounded him; then they led him farther, stopping at the driveway entrance to the Firth mansion.

"It's all right then," Annie declared. "They must have Teddy down there. Someone was able to stop him."

But Jonathan felt sick with dread. Something about the way the lanterns had closed around Grandpa made him think the worst.

Only what was the worst? What could have happened? Ignoring Mrs. Noone's order to keep back, Jonathan pelted down the hill toward the cluster of lights. By the time he reached them, he had to push through a small crowd before he saw the wagon tipped on its side.

"Too heavy," someone yelled. "Empty it out."

"First see to the horse!" another person directed.

"Capewell's here."

Something large was thrown from the wagon, followed by other objects. A man cursed as glass plates dropped from a holder tossed upside down. Shattered glass crunched underfoot. People warned one another to watch out for nails, for splintered wood.

"Somebody bring a pistol," a man called out.

"On its way. Mr. Firth's been sent for," came a reply.

"Horse break a leg?" someone asked.

"Can't tell yet. He's just being unhitched."

Jonathan scooted around behind the rear of the wagon. It had hit the granite pillar so hard that it had slammed sideways against the ornamental wall. One broken shaft had pinned Teddy to the ground. His head was stretched out, his mouth wide and gasping, as if he had only now stopped running. Grandpa and two other men bent over him, pulling at fastenings, calling for more light, speaking among themselves to loosen this and raise that.

The crowd parted for a small man in a frock coat, who knelt beside Teddy, placed a hand on his throat, and then tapped above the staring eye. If he was a doctor, thought Jonathan, he would be able to help.

"Capewell," the man said, "how did this come about?"

Grandpa, a leather strap in his mouth, only grunted as he tugged at a buckle.

"Inexcusable!" the man declared.

"The horse had been tied," someone told him.

"During the fireworks? That's sheer negligence."

"It is not!" Annie cried, thrusting forward to confront the

man. "Uncle Rodney has never neglected his horse, and Teddy was used to fireworks. He never bolted before."

"Annie!" Mrs. Noone called from somewhere behind.

"That's your opinion, young lady, but someone brought the poor creature to this sad state. He'll probably have to be destroyed."

"No!" she shrieked. "We can take care of him. We'll heal him."

The man said, "I applaud your determination, young lady. But it's no excuse for bad manners."

At this point Mrs. Noone reached Annie "You must beg Mr. Firth's pardon," she said. Then she dropped to her knees beside the horse. "Oh, Rodney," she said, "I didn't realize—"

By now only the collar, surcingle, and crupper remained, but the horse made no attempt to move. Every breath he drew rasped painfully. Jonathan was shoved aside and had to find another place, this time close to Teddy's head. He fingered the ribbons still braided in Teddy's forelock.

Grandpa told Jonathan to step back. He spoke softly, as if the fireworks were not blasting the night sky, as if no one else stood by, as if he were far from this place.

Jonathan backed onto glass and other debris. Nearly tripping over a mangled prop, he glanced up and caught sight of two men emptying the wagon. One of them looked like Mr. Whittaker, but without direct light Jonathan couldn't be sure. As soon as the shot was fired, the two men paused. Then they went back to unloading the wagon so that it could be righted.

Jonathan made his way forward again. Several men had just dragged the dead horse clear of the wreck. Grandpa said to no one in particular, "I was looking at the wrong thing." He dropped down beside the splayed body and ran his hand under the surcingle. Jonathan was reminded of all those times that Grandpa had checked like that to make sure Teddy wasn't getting rubbed and sore from harness pressure and sweat.

When Grandpa withdrew his hand, it was smeared with blood.

"What is it?" Jonathan asked. "What happened?"

"It's a wound," Grandpa said, his voice dry and flat. "Blew a hole right through him. I saw enough of this kind of injury to last a lifetime. Smell it," he told Jonathan.

"What?" said Jonathan, recoiling.

"Go on. Put your face right down there to Teddy's belly and get a good whiff of that, and don't you ever forget it."

There was no escape. Jonathan crouched low. Only one lantern remained near the carcass. Trying to avoid contact with the wound, Jonathan drew closer and breathed in. He smelled hot blood first, and then, at the same time, the unmistakable reek of scorched skin and hair.

He lurched back on his heels, gulping the night air.

22

By the time Jonathan came downstairs the next morning, Grandpa had already gone to the livery stable to make arrangements for getting Teddy's carcass removed and his wagon attended to. Jonathan borrowed Annie's bicycle to ride through town and back up to the accident scene. There was the wagon, but the horse had already been loaded onto the knacker's cart and hauled away.

The wagon was propped on two wheels, with timbers holding it upright. The other wheels lay on equipment thrown aside to lighten the load. Slowly Jonathan began to pick things over, sorting whatever he thought might be saved or repaired. What was to be done with one of the spare horseshoes that Grandpa always kept in the wagon for emergencies? They fitted Teddy's hooves. Jonathan carried it from one heap to another. Was it trash now?

He was recovering camera parts when he heard a horse approach. Looking up, he saw Mr. Firth riding toward him. Mr. Firth reined in his horse and said, "You're Capewell's grandson?"

Jonathan straightened. "Yes, sir."

"I'm doubtful that was an accident. Does anyone hold a grudge against your grandfather?"

Jonathan shook his head. "I don't believe so. Mrs. Noone thinks someone may have been throwing firecrackers."

"I'd like to know who would do that to a horse. I'd have something to say about it before I turned them over to the constable. I think I'll put up a reward."

Jonathan said, "Yes, sir."

"It'll be costly for your grandfather, I imagine," Mr. Firth remarked. "I suppose that rig held most of his worldly goods."

Jonathan said, "I don't know. I don't think he knows. Right now he's just seeing to what has to be done. Teddy was his horse for a long, long time."

"I expect it will be hard for him to carry on now. And what about you? Are you studying to be a photographer like your grandfather?"

"I'm supposed to learn about it. But before I came away with him, I used to want to be a detective more than anything. I don't know."

Mr. Firth leaned down from the saddle and spoke in a low, conspiratorial tone. "Well, here's a bit of detection for you. Go back to where the horse was tied. Walk every step of the way he went, and then tell me what you think."

"Now?"

"Yes, boy, now! Run up there and look around; then follow the hoof and wheel prints."

"But there were other wagons," Jonathan protested.

"Right you are. See if you can find the very ones that landed here. Now run."

Jonathan thought the little man with the pink face was a bit odd, but he had an air of authority about him that made Jonathan set aside the camera parts and jog up toward the field.

It was not quite back to normal. The serving tables, boards on sawhorses like Mrs. Noone's counter, had not yet been carried away. There were some barrels, a few milk cans, piles of wood chips, and flags staking out areas for contests and games.

What should he look at then? Grandpa's wagon had left dents in the grass, and there was a bare patch along the wire fence where Teddy had grazed when his tether was lengthened. What was left of the rope now? Jonathan looked, then took hold of it and stared at the broken end. Not broken. It didn't have the frayed look of a rope that broke. It had been cut clean through.

He couldn't follow the wheel tracks out of the field. The ground was too chewed up by many wheels, shod hooves, and feet. But a little farther on, the wheels left the track and dug in hard, and here he was able to see the deep indentations made by a plunging horse. He started to follow these clear marks, then suddenly reversed to make sure he could tell where they began.

It was easy to retrace Teddy's path as it veered in crazy loops, a terrible, cutting sepentine that crashed into the pillar, where Mr. Firth on his horse awaited Jonathan.

"Well?" said Mr. Firth. "What did you see? What do you think?"

Jonathan tried to rub the tears from his eyes, but they wouldn't stop. "It must have hurt him so," he said in a choked voice. "No one ever hurt him. Until this."

"Was it an accident?"

Jonathan shook his head. "The rope was cut."

"Yes. That's what made me doubt that it was an accident. What else?"

"It happened after he was outside the field."

"Go on," Mr. Firth told him.

"Someone led him out first. It was on purpose. Then they did that awful thing to him. But there's no way to tell whether it was a prank or mean on purpose."

"Does it matter?" Mr. Firth demanded.

Jonathan had to think a moment. How would a sleuth on the trail of a criminal answer that question? "Yes, it makes a difference what sort of person you'd look for."

"I believe you might be a detective after all," Mr. Firth declared. "I'll speak to Constable Stebbins because I won't tolerate cruelty to helpless animals. Meanwhile, since you know a deal about your grandfather, see what you can come up with."

Jonathan shook his head. "I didn't even know that fireworks remind him of the war. And what happened to Teddy, that reminds him, too."

"I seldom apologize, but I'm bound to say I owe him an apology," Mr. Firth declared. He turned and rode away, leaving Jonathan surrounded by the debris from Grandpa's studio wagon.

23

Jonathan was still sorting through the debris when a man drove a two-wheeled dump cart up to the wagon to load whatever parts needed repair. Then Grandpa arrived with two volunteers, one of them Mr. Whittaker. They brought gunnysacks and a shovel and rake.

"The simplest thing," Mr. Whittaker said, "would be to dig a hole right here and bury the entire mess."

The dump cart man said he wouldn't recommend that without first getting Mr. Firth's permission. But no one seemed to want to seek that out, so they went to work loading things into the sacks. They talked just a little, mostly wondering out loud why anyone would play such a cruel prank. It didn't seem to cross their minds that the mischief might have been planned.

When the dump cart was full, the driver set off down the hill to the carriage works. The others kept on bagging, Grandpa repeatedly warning them to watch out for shards of glass. He had already cut both his hands, though that didn't stop him from picking up every splinter he could find.

Jonathan suddenly remembered the tintype in his pocket. The picture of the monkey for Annie was to have been a reminder of the Glorious Fourth. He fished it out of his pocket and dropped it in a gunnysack full of the broken glass.

Mr. Whittaker held up an almost complete negative plate with a jagged crack through it. "Is this worth saving?" he asked.

Grandpa glanced at it, then shook his head. "But save the holders, the containers. Some of my best photographs were in the wagon. One of them might have survived."

"I doubt there are any plates left in the holders," Mr. Whittaker replied. "I'm afraid I'm partly to blame. You see, last night we were in such a hurry to right the wagon and try to save the horse that I just threw everything out that I could grab."

"I appreciate that," Grandpa said. "I'm grateful for what you tried to do."

"Still, I'm sorry I've added to your losses, Rodney. And mine. I don't suppose you're holding out much hope for those river pictures."

"River pictures," Grandpa repeated musingly. "No, it was other negatives, fine ones, that are all smashed here. I'm pretty sure the river plates weren't in the wagon."

"Ah," said Mr. Whittaker with a sharp intake of breath, "I thought . . . I was under the impression . . ." His words trailed off.

Jonathan couldn't help noticing the way Mr. Whittaker

faltered. As if in a daze, he let the plate fall to the ground where it broke apart along the crack line.

"Try the gunnysack," the other volunteer suggested.

Mr. Whittaker quickly stooped to retrieve the two pieces. He worked in silence, giving Jonathan time to wonder what he had observed in that exchange with Grandpa.

By the time the dump cart returned, most of the gunny-sacks were full and ready for loading. Some of them were so lumpy that they tended to snag or stick to roots and stones. But grabbing them to lift them off the ground was danger-ous and could give the hauler a mean poke or cut right through the fabric.

Grandpa told Jonathan to leave this part of the work to the men, who were tall enough to raise the sacks a bit as they moved them along. So Jonathan leaned up against the wagon, half his mind on what he had learned about the acci-dent, the other half observing the men dragging the sacks of refuse up into the cart.

Something protruded from Mr. Whittaker's sack. Each time it dug into the ground and drew him up short, he had to give it a hard kick. Jonathan was only mildly interested in this routine. Then Mr. Whittaker lost patience with the thing. Using sheer force, he yanked the protrusion side-ways, ripping the sack.

All at once Jonathan was extremely interested in what he was looking at. It was like yesterday's double exposure, only this time he was seeing the man in the checked shirt strug-gling with an upturned boat and then with a stubborn sack that resisted his frenzied efforts to send it over the rapids.

Jonathan's heart thudded; the roar of the rapids echoed in

his ears. He was still leaning against the broken wagon. He hadn't moved. Yet he was as breathless as if he had just run all the way through town and up to Firth Field.

Mr. Whittaker heaved the torn gunnysack up to Grandpa, then walked back for the last one. "Something wrong?" he asked Jonathan as he passed by.

Jonathan sucked in air, nearly gagging as Mr. Whittaker reached toward him, extending his hand. Through a blur Jonathan caught a glimpse of a scorched cuff, the inside of the wrist seared red. All at once the smell of Teddy's singed hair and burned skin came rushing back to him. Then Grandpa took Mr. Whittaker's place beside Jonathan, ordering him to ride down into town with the dump cart driver and then go straight home as promptly as possible.

"I'm all right," Jonathan said. "I want to stay with you."

"You do what you're told," Grandpa retorted. "It's been a hard night and day."

Mr. Whittaker said, "Your grandfather's right, young man. He doesn't need anything more going wrong just now."

Grandpa hoisted Annie's bicycle onto the cart. Feeling hot and queasy, Jonathan climbed up on the seat beside the cart driver. Part of him couldn't wait to get away from this place. Part of him resisted being sent. He needed to talk to Grandpa. But he also needed to think things through.

How could Jonathan tell Grandpa what he had seen and smelled if he wasn't sure himself? Was it possible that the impressions flashing at him were the product of an excited imagination? If only he could make sense of it all.

24

Mrs. Noone said Jonathan looked peaky and ought to take it easy. "It's natural to be grieving over Teddy," she said to him. "You've had a shock."

Annie eyed him but didn't say anything.

Later she brought him a new dime novel, *Honest Harry, or the Country Boy Adrift in the City.* "Ma knew all along that some of these are sold with magazines in the tobacco shop. She just didn't want me reading them. But she told me I could buy this one to help you get your mind off what happened."

Jonathan, who had raced through *A Tale of Two Cities,* was well into *Bleak House.* He thanked Annie and told her she might as well read *Honest Harry* while she could. He could get to it after she had gone. Casting an anxious glance in the direction of the kitchen, she slipped out before her mother caught her leaving with it.

A few minutes later Jonathan looked up from his book and glanced out the window to discover his grandfather stopped in front of the house. In one hand he held a glass plate holder. He seemed to be uncertain where to put it, but he made no move to enter the shed. Nor did he come close to the front door.

Jonathan put the book down and went out to him. Grandpa seemed in a fog, slow to notice Jonathan, slow to recall why he had sent his grandson home.

"Are you all right?" Jonathan asked.

Grandpa nodded. "People have been kind."

"Grandpa," Jonathan said, diving in despite the fog, "do you know who Mr. Whittaker is?"

Grandpa looked at Jonathan. "Why, of course. What do you mean?"

"Have you any idea why he's so keen for your river pictures?"

Grandpa nodded. "He's establishing a tour for rusticators who want to experience the wilderness, only not on the grand scale of that hotel on Moosehead Lake that's all got up with gas lights and bathrooms. He's providing more rustic accommodations, but with some comforts to go with views of the river runs."

Jonathan seized on the river reference. "Has he mentioned being where we were? Is that why he wants those pictures?"

Grandpa shrugged. "Maybe he has. I don't recall."

"I think we saw him there." Except Grandpa had seen him for only a moment.

"Really? I'd be surprised. He would have said so."

"Not if he doesn't want you to know he was there then."

"What are you saying, boy? Why should he care one way or the other?"

"Don't you remember that man in the checked shirt? You thought he was trying to shift the roof out of the way so the logs wouldn't jam up on the rapids. What if he's that man? What if he did something . . . bad and is afraid your pictures will show it?"

Grandpa scowled. "All this excitement has gone to your head," he said.

"No, I'm not excited." But he was. He could feel himself heating up again. He had seen enough of the man in the checked shirt to recognize certain gestures. Now that Jonathan gave voice to his thoughts, they began to come together. "He's hiding something. He might be the one . . . I think he's maybe the person who set Teddy off."

"Now that's enough!" Grandpa exclaimed. "I don't know what's got into you, but I'll hear no more against a man who has been uncommonly kind."

"Too kind," Jonathan shot back. "From the start. Too kind, too interested. And now, Grandpa, he thinks you may still have those pictures. Evidence."

"Evidence!" Grandpa snorted. "You read too many detective stories. Evidence about what?"

"I don't know exactly. But it has to do with that morning at the river. He's afraid of what the camera might have recorded. He thought the plates were still in the wagon because I thought they were. I told him. He must have arranged the accident to destroy them."

"Jonathan!" Grandpa exclaimed. "That's a terrible accusation against a civil gentleman. Whoever set off firecrackers under Teddy was a careless brute. I confess that I found Fred's persistence a bit irritating at first, but he's a decent fellow who has gone out of his way to save a poor beast and to help me."

Jonathan said, "Whoever did it, Grandpa, wasn't careless at all. It was planned, and I can prove—"

Grandpa placed his hands on Jonathan's shoulders. Squeezing hard, he said, "I want to put an end to this right now. It's nonsense. It's evil. It shames me."

"But there's more!" Jonathan blurted, desperate to draw Grandpa's attention to Mr. Whittaker's seared skin and scorched cuff.

"No, there is not. No more," Grandpa commanded, spinning Jonathan around and propelling him into the house.

"What are you two up to?" Mrs. Noone asked. "Lunch is on the table."

"We've been finishing a conversation," Grandpa told her.

"Good," she said, "because I want to begin a fresh one with you. And I hope you'll let me persuade you of my good idea."

What Mrs. Noone proposed was that Grandpa accompany them on the trip to Grandmother's relatives. "You need a change, Rodney," she urged. "Even after your wagon is repaired, it will take awhile to ready it as a traveling studio."

"I may put off all that," Grandpa replied. "I may not be able to travel the fair route this year. I don't know how long it will take to get new equipment shipped here, and after I pay for it and for the wagon, I may not be able to afford a new horse. So I might just stay put, keep the gallery open."

"It's only for a few days," Mrs. Noone said to him. "And you've always wanted to photograph Grandmother's relatives."

"Still got shadow-catcher?" Grandmother asked.

Grandpa nodded. "Thank goodness the monster camera was in the studio."

"You bring him. I show many things."

"Please come, Uncle Rodney," Annie begged. She turned to Jonathan. "We stop more often when he's with us."

"I know," Jonathan said. If Grandpa went with them, Jonathan might find a way to catch out Mr. Whittaker in his deception. If only he could find out what had been in the gunnysack that the man in the checked shirt had struggled with that morning. For all Jonathan knew, it could have been a body. Was there some simple clue back then that he had let slip from his grasp?

Being a detective was less like scrambling for arrowheads than he had once thought. Of course you picked up a lot of small stones before you found a perfect handmade flint. But when you trudged through a freshly turned field with your eyes cast down to the furrows, at least you knew what you were looking for. Solving a crime was a lot different. First you had to realize that one had been committed, and by that time the clues might be thoroughly buried.

Grandpa said, "You can't fit so many of us and my equipment in your buggy."

"Since when have you failed to invent ways to load on extra gear?" Annie's mother demanded with a smile. "It will be a challenge. That's what you need just now. Get your mind off your losses."

"And you?" he asked, sending her a long look. "The best

negatives are destroyed. The ones you've been after me to print again. You were right."

"I'm not interested in who was right and who wrong," she told him, rising. "Let's just pick up the pieces as best we can." She began to clear the table.

25

Annie, rubbing linseed oil into the harness, said, "Ruby's been restless all day. Not the way she is when Uncle Rodney usually goes away. She acts as if she knows Teddy's not coming back."

Jonathan kept sponging one section of Ruby's collar. "She's just restless," he said.

"You're not even listening to me," Annie complained. "You're not paying attention to anything."

Jonathan said, "Annie, please help me. Grandpa ought to go with you. I have to stay here."

"Why?"

"It's about Mr. Whittaker." He told her all he had learned but didn't mention what had crossed his mind about the contents of the gunnysack dumped in the river.

"It's like a real detective story," she said almost gleefully. "Shouldn't Uncle Rodney be right here where he can keep an eye on his pictures?"

"He won't protect them. He thinks I'm making all this up. At least if he's gone I can hide the plates, keep them safe until—" Jonathan faltered.

"Until what?" Annie asked him.

"I don't know exactly. In dime novels a detective finds a way to trip up the suspect, trick him into confessing. Maybe something like that."

"What about Mr. Firth?" Annie suggested. "He put you on to those clues about Teddy. Shouldn't you tell him all this?"

Jonathan shook his head. The thought of walking up to that imposing house and asking to speak with Mr. Firth was just too daunting. "Not now," he said. "Not yet. Maybe after Grandpa leaves with you."

"First, though, we need to convince Uncle Rodney to print those pictures," Annie said. "Then you'll be sure."

But Jonathan doubted that. "Most of the time the camera was facing the other way. Upriver. Besides, even if Mr. Whittaker shows up in one, it won't amount to evidence because we don't know why he was doing what I saw. I was watching most of the time, and I still don't know what was really happening."

Jonathan fell silent, recalling the frantic efforts of the man in the checked shirt. Then he said, "But he hasn't wanted us to know he was there where the Indian was supposed to be. The men in camp said that jam above the rapids was hard to pick, the kind that calls for at least four men and two boats. The Indian was ordered to do it alone, only he wasn't there. But Mr. Whittaker was. He was trying to get the boat and the gunnysack over the rapids ahead of the logs, before the drivers came. He acted as though he thought he was all by himself."

"Are you certain the Indian wasn't there?"

"Pretty sure. Some of the loggers guessed he'd run off,

but they were worried about him. A few went to look for him."

"Do you think that upside-down boat was his?" Annie asked.

Jonathan said, "Whose else could it have been? And I can't be sure, but I think there was a crack in it. Anyway, it vanished. Downriver, I suppose. Over the rapids."

"Well," Annie declared, "we have to see the pictures. Ma can make Uncle Rodney develop them. For weeks now she's been waiting for new prints from the good negative plates, the ones that got smashed with the wagon. She sent the first prints all the way to New York, and she needed another set. She says it's a terrible loss. So she might get him to print the river photographs before something happens to them, too. I'll talk to her." Annie tossed the rag at Jonathan and ran out of the barn.

Jonathan passed a critical eye over Ruby's collar. A small section of it was beautifully clean. The rest of it was still a bit grimy. He carried it and the soapy water out into the sunshine, where he applied himself to cleaning the leather and keeping from going over and over the questions that swarmed like mosquitoes around his head.

Eventually Grandpa called him to help bring the buggy out to the street. Then Grandpa beckoned him into the shed. "Miranda thinks I should get a start with some of these pictures," he said. "But since you ought to begin developing and printing real photographs soon, you might as well try your hand with one of these."

Jonathan covered the two windows while Grandpa poured pyrogallic acid into a tray. He would use self-toning paper to save time, but he wanted Jonathan to understand that a fine glass plate negative deserves a print toned the old way. That called for careful mixing of chemicals and six changes of water to remove the silver salts from the exposed surface. "You can never be too cautious," he insisted. "Two minutes of sunlight is enough, then open your frame in dim light to check. When your print is ready, agitate it in the fixer bath for ten minutes, rinse thoroughly, then bathe it in a hypo-clearing solution. After that a full hour, no less, of washing before you let it air-dry."

"No wonder you don't do it that way often," Jonathan said, wishing Grandpa would forget the instructing and finish the prints.

"It makes a finer picture," Grandpa said. "It all depends on whether you want a quick sale or something to make you proud. Remember, Jonathan, when you work with silver bromide or silver chloride, the exposed silver salts turn black as they form the image, but the unexposed grains remain, and if they aren't washed away, they'll darken when the print is exposed to light and blot out your image. The hypo, the fixer, washes away those silver grains, but then the fixer itself must be removed. Otherwise the sulfur in it tarnishes the image."

Jonathan nodded a lot and tried to look interested. But when the first emerging print showed the empty river, it brought everything back: the roaring rapids, the fog, the small drama of the man in the checked shirt.

Maybe not so small.

Grandpa hovered over the bench as Jonathan agitated the tray for the next print. Neither of them spoke, but Jonathan knew that Grandpa didn't quite trust him and was afraid he might rush the process. As it was, his fingers were already stained from the solution. That made him think of Mr. Whittaker again and the brown, jagged edge of his shirt cuff and his burned skin. But now that Grandpa had given Jonathan this much responsibility for an important picture, it wasn't the time to raise the subject of Mr. Whittaker.

The third print, more blurred than the previous ones, showed the view toward the rapids and part of the roof. Jonathan was so thrilled to see that extraordinary apparition again that for a second he forgot what he was looking for. But there, in the upper right corner, was the man in the checked shirt. Jonathan gazed at the picture as hard as he could, willing it to reveal more than it did. The river spray obstructed the image, and anyhow, the figure was too small and contorted to be identified.

Grandpa, satisfied with what he saw, commenced to print one more picture. There wouldn't be time to develop more than these today. At least it was a start, a few photographs for Mr. Whittaker, who had been so thoughtful and kind, and a few to placate Miranda Noone, who was so dismayed at the loss of the special negative plates she set such store by.

Grandpa didn't point to the tiny image of the man in the checked shirt. He didn't mention Mr. Whittaker's name either. He just concluded his lesson with a lecture on the thrifty practice of washing all negative plates that weren't worth keeping. Once they were perfectly clean, they could be stored in a holder for future use.

26

Annie advised Jonathan not to mention staying home until his grandfather was fully settled in his own mind about going with the Noones. She also advised Jonathan to offer to help out in the store while the Noones were away.

He chose a good time to speak to Annie's mother. She was frowning as she tried to stow some extra things in the buggy for Grandmother. And Grandpa, who had gone downtown to lock up the gallery, would probably return with more equipment.

"You wouldn't mind being here by yourself?" she asked.

"Not at all."

"Well, thank you, Jonathan. I'm relieved to know we'll have some backup in the store. I'll speak to Rodney."

To Jonathan's surprise, Grandpa didn't take long to be convinced. He made a few perfunctory remarks about having promised Jonathan's parents to look out for him and then agreed with Mrs. Noone that it would be a good experience for a growing boy who would soon have to look out for himself.

Early the next morning, just before the departure, Grandpa proceeded to list a few leftover tasks, mostly deliveries, that Jonathan should see to in the next few days. Among them was an instruction to mount the four river prints Grandpa had left in the shed to dry and make them available to Mr. Whittaker, who would find a note to that effect on the gallery door.

"I wish I could stay home, too," Annie blurted. "May I?"

Jonathan glared at her. If she put up any kind of fuss, Grandpa might change his mind.

Mrs. Noone sent a sharp look toward the house. "I'm glad you didn't ask that in your grandmother's hearing," she said. "And I think you know the answer."

Annie flushed. "I didn't mean—" she began to explain.

But her mother shook her head and raised a finger to her lips as Grandmother approached with a basket of her belongings.

Annie drew Jonathan aside. "You must go to Mr. Firth. You'll have to speak up, you know. You can't be shy when it's a matter of life and death."

"I guess so," Jonathan said, without admitting that he was terrified of approaching that house on the hill by himself.

After they had driven off, he went into the shed, where he found that Grandpa had left things in disarray. For a moment he felt overwhelmed. Was this a sign that Grandpa's mind was unraveling? Or was this mess no worse than the carelessness Mrs. Noone so often complained of?

She always made a distinction between Grandpa's precise and patient photography and his occasional disregard of practical matters. Just last evening she had insisted that he bring only dry plates on the journey. Then she had assailed him all over again for leaving those special negative plates at risk in the wagon. Grandpa had reminded her that he had often carried glass over rough terrain without a problem. No one would have predicted that anything bad could happen in Firth Field.

Jonathan shook his head. Had they been alert, he and Grandpa, they might have predicted some kind of mischief and prevented the disaster. The words Grandpa had muttered when he happened upon Teddy's mortal wound came back to Jonathan: "I was looking at the wrong thing."

All along they had been looking at the wrong thing.

Jonathan had time to clean up the trays and mount the photographs before going down the hill to the store. He spent a long time gazing at the image of the man in the checked shirt. If only something in the picture were the clue he was looking for, something that would supply a reason for the man's strange behavior. Was there another exposure, as yet undeveloped, that would reveal that clue?

He gathered up the full holders and took them into Grandmother's shed. Grandpa would develop and print them as soon as he returned, but meanwhile it wouldn't hurt to tuck them away behind ash splints and long strips of basswood bark.

After that Jonathan took the print of the rapids upstairs, peered once more at the image of the man, and realized that what he had taken for shadow must be the beard he now recalled seeing. He thought for a moment. A beard was an easy identifying mark and easy to alter. If Mr. Whittaker had shaved his off just before coming to Masham, that was another indication that he wanted to avoid recognition.

It had worked, too. On Decoration Day Mr. Whittaker, without face hair, had passed that test with two people who must have seen him just a few weeks earlier. That left only the threat of what the camera had seen.

Jonathan was about to shove the print under his mattress when he saw that Annie had left *Honest Harry* on it. So he slid the picture inside the dime novel. Concealing it between the pages of a detective story gave him a boost, even though he wasn't sure why he was hiding it.

He still didn't have a plan, only the sense that it was important to hold this in reserve. After all, it might prove to be important for Mr. Whittaker to believe that one other picture existed, a picture with a man in it.

27

Jonathan put off calling on Mr. Firth until the end of the following day. All the way up the hill he rehearsed the points he needed to make. If only his growling stomach didn't make itself heard. But if he had gone home first for his supper of cold leftovers, he would have had two steep hills to climb instead of the one. He had already run his feet off delivering finished prints for Grandpa and parcels for the store.

When he came to the granite pillars, he stopped for a second to collect himself. The slanting sun speared the trampled ground and edged the depression in the grass where Teddy had fallen. Jonathan could still see him, ribbons and all, and how the lantern had shown his lips drawn back from the long yellow teeth. That hideous grin had borne no resemblance to the gentle mouth Jonathan had bitted so often.

He walked up the long driveway, slowing as he neared the house. At the door he reached for the brass knocker.

"I have information for Mr. Firth," he said to the austere-looking woman who answered his knock. Was she Mrs. Firth? "I'm Jonathan Capewell."

"Is Mr. Firth expecting you?" she asked.

"Yes. No. Not this very minute, but sometime."

She said, "Mr. Firth is at dinner. I'll tell him you're here." She shut the door.

When it opened again, wider this time, she beckoned him into the front hall, which was larger and grander even than Mrs. Noone's parlor. He paused beside a tall porcelain umbrella stand containing a brilliant blue-and-green peacock feather and a cane with a silver fox handle.

"In here," the woman said, conducting Jonathan into a dining room with dark curtains covering the windows and oil paintings in gilded frames on the wall.

Mr. Firth, who sat alone at the table, beckoned Jonathan toward a chair. "I could tell right off you were quick witted," he declared cheerfully, "but this is even quicker than I expected. I assume you have come with information?"

Jonathan tried not to look at the beef stew on Mr. Firth's plate. "I don't have proof," he said, "but I'm nearly certain that I know who caused the accident, and the culprit may be guilty of something even worse."

"Culprit, indeed!" Mr. Firth declared. "You speak like a seasoned sleuth." He raised a forkful of beef and potato, and Jonathan's eyes followed its progress to his mouth. "I assume you've dined already?" Mr. Firth said.

"I worked in Mrs. Noone's store today," Jonathan told him. "I came straight here."

"Mrs. Rhinebeck," Mr. Firth called, "this young man will join me for supper."

Jonathan didn't know how to refuse without giving offense, so he didn't try to. He simply thanked Mr. Firth and then the woman, who set a place and brought him a full plate. But it was hard to eat and talk and recall his rehearsed order of things.

Mr. Firth helped out by asking questions about Grandpa and the store that called for simple answers. Jonathan paused after every mouthful so that he could respond briefly and politely. All the while he made an effort to keep his head clear.

It wasn't until the luscious strawberries were eaten and Mr. Firth was sipping his coffee that Jonathan bore down on his case. "It goes back to the river drive," he said. "Where they're logging. We were there. Grandpa didn't see everything I saw because he aimed his camera the other way."

"Where is this leading?" Mr. Firth asked. He didn't sound impatient, but he seemed to be nudging Jonathan toward a conclusion.

Jonathan didn't see how he could bring Mr. Firth to that point without adequate background. "It's all part of what happened here on the Fourth," he said.

Mr. Firth swirled the coffee in the bottom of his cup and called for more.

Jonathan resumed his account of the man in the checked shirt.

Mr. Firth interrupted him. "But you didn't see anything wrong, so what does it amount to?"

"The man came here to Masham afterward," Jonathan said. "He came looking for pictures Grandpa took that day. He's been trying to get ahold of them, and I think it's because he doesn't want anyone to know he was where he was, doing what he was doing."

"Which is what?" Mr. Firth demanded.

"Shoving that upside-down boat over the rapids, and after that a gunnysack full of . . . I don't know what. It might have been someone's gear. At least that's what it looked to be. Or maybe it held something else," Jonathan added cautiously. "He must have known the logs and the river drivers were coming. He freed the boat and sent it along just before the roof showed. I haven't told you about the roof yet. It sailed downriver from the lake and fetched up on the rapids. It nearly blocked the river drive."

"I'm following some of this," Mr. Firth said, "but for the life of me I can't see how any of it connects with sticking firecrackers on a horse and setting them off."

"It's that man," Jonathan said. "It's him. Mr. Whittaker."

"What? Fred Whittaker?" Mr. Firth set down his cup with a clatter. His pink face grew pinker.

"It is. He was after the pictures that he thought were in the wagon."

"He wouldn't do such a thing!" Mr. Firth exclaimed. "I know the man. He would never torture a poor horse to gain some kind of advantage. He's not guilty of anything like that. You're quite right that he's been in the woods and on the river. I grant you that much. It was clever of you to guess that Fred might be the man you saw."

"He is. I didn't recognize him right off. He'd shaved his beard."

"There's no crime in that. A lot of the men make a clean-faced start after spending the winter in the woods. You can't invent a crime where none exists. No, my boy, you'll have to start all over again if you're going to solve this puzzle."

Jonathan sat in silence, a confusion of questions and retorts boiling in his head.

Mr. Firth said, "You'd better rein in your vivid imagination, too."

"Has Mr. Whittaker told you what he was doing that morning on the rapids?" Jonathan asked.

"Why should he? There were many mornings for him, not just the one you witnessed. And misinterpreted. He may have been there. As foreman he had—"

"Foreman? He was the boss?" Jonathan exclaimed. "That's it! The boss sent the Indian to handle the backlog alone. That Indian, Muskrat Mac, he didn't want to go. It was too dangerous. The other loggers were afraid for him, too."

Mr. Firth was nodding. That gave Jonathan hope that he was changing his mind. But Mr. Firth said, "It doesn't surprise me. Those Indians can be surly and stubborn. When they take it into their heads to turn down a job, they make trouble for the whole drive, and it's up to the foreman to hold to a schedule. I can assure you there's almost always two points of view in situations like that."

"Some loggers went looking for Muskrat Mac because he didn't come back."

"Did you see the Indian there that morning?"

"No, sir."

"No, of course not. You saw a man who might or might not have been Fred Whittaker. The camera may reveal the man's identity. If I ask Fred, I've no doubt he'll come right out and tell me. Even if the Indian had been there; supposing he had come to grief through his own resistance to the foreman's order, there's no proof that Fred contributed to the trouble. For all you know you were witness to a failed rescue attempt by a man you may or may not be able to recognize."

Mr. Firth pushed back his chair and stood up. Jonathan could see that he was being dismissed. Rising to his feet, he was conscious of this powerful man's slight build, his mild, almost scrubbed look. Why, then, was he so intimidating?

Mr. Firth said, "Fred Whittaker had river experience before I sent him north to speed up this year's timber production. He's an enterprising fellow and completely frank with me. When I hired him as foreman, I knew he meant to scout out places and people to set up a tour business. I'd no objection so long as he delivered the logs."

"Doesn't it count that the men in camp think he risked their lives?"

"River driving is a most dangerous employment," Mr. Firth replied as he ushered Jonathan toward the hall. "Almost every year there are injuries and deaths. A man's body fetched up on rocks not too long ago. Such losses are always regrettable, but that's how it is. You'll find grave markers all along these rivers. The drivers know the chances when they take up their work." He paused, then added, "I'm glad you spoke to me about your suspicions because I can keep them between us. You don't want your grandfather disgraced on top of all he's been through."

Jonathan said that he didn't.

"What does he make of your extraordinary notion?"

"Not much," Jonathan mumbled.

Mr. Firth said, "Well, then. A reasonable man. Not given to flinging baseless charges around. Though I know you mean no harm. I'll talk with Fred Whittaker if that will ease your mind. I think you'll find that he has a sound reason for seeking those pictures. And don't you give up, boy. We'll find the real culprit."

Jonathan walked away from the grand house perplexed and defeated. He no longer knew what to believe. Mr. Firth's rejection undermined his confidence in his own judgment. Had he ever truly made sense of those senseless events, or must he do what Mr. Firth recommended and start all over putting the blasted pieces together?

28

With lamp in hand Jonathan went up to bed. The house felt strange in its silence. He didn't want to think anymore. Finding the dime novel where he had left it, he considered losing himself in the story of Honest Harry, the country boy adrift in the city. Jonathan mused that he wasn't so different, a country boy, too, and out of his depth.

He flipped through the pages, and the photograph fell out. Once again he scrutinized the scene. He held the lamp low, and its flame sputtered a moment, giving the image something akin to a lifelike spasm. That brought back what he had actually seen, the man struggling frantically to send the overturned boat and then the gunnysack over the rapids. Was Jonathan wrong to suspect that this was to conceal a crime? He had not been mistaken about what he had seen. That much he knew. And if he wasn't mistaken about that, then didn't it follow that he might not be mistaken about the rest?

Relief rushed into him. He hadn't mentioned this photograph. Even if it was only a small scrap of evidence, it might be enough to catch a man in a lie. Meanwhile it was safe, in his possession. Not a shadow, he told himself, a beard. Thanks to the camera, the true shadow-catcher, the identity of that figure was not in doubt.

But what had Mr. Whittaker been up to? If he hadn't injured or murdered the Indian, he wouldn't care about a picture showing him bending over that boat. So all Jonathan needed to do was find out which picture Mr. Whittaker sought.

Throughout the next day Jonathan kept an eye out for him. Twice he ran upstairs to check the message Grandpa had left pinned to the gallery door with Mr. Whittaker's name on it. But there it remained, apparently untouched, unread.

Jonathan found this puzzling. After all, Mr. Whittaker had learned that the river pictures had not been in the wagon after all. So what prevented him from making another attempt to get them?

If Mr. Firth had been in touch with Mr. Whittaker, would that have scared him off? There was only one way to find out if the two men had spoken, but Jonathan shied away from another session in the house at the top of the hill. Besides, he was beginning to enjoy his new routine, working in the store with Ernie, then, during the long, light evenings, exploring the nearby countryside on Annie's bicycle or reading into the night without interruption.

Honest Harry didn't hold his attention. Or maybe its predictable detective plot brought his mind back to Mr. Whittaker's puzzling absence, distracting him and starting him thinking again, trying to plug the holes in the narrative that connected the events that led to Teddy's death and the wagon wreck.

But there were other books in the parlor, thick novels on the shelf next to those by Dickens. Jonathan could almost see and hear some of the characters he read about. They drew him into their worlds so utterly that he imagined them as real people caught unaware by some hidden camera, and for a while he was able to forget the worries that plagued him. Then a book by Mark Twain opened his eyes to what he had looked at but not seen.

At first the book seemed all adventure. But the more he read about Huck Finn and Jim, who was a runaway slave, the more he was struck by an undercurrent in their world that paralleled his own. If a man was discounted because he was a slave or an Indian, he could then be considered expendable. When Mr. Firth implied that Muskrat Mac wasn't worth worrying about, wasn't he expressing that view, one that must distort the millowner's own interpretation of events?

Jonathan renewed his efforts to master the facts, to discover clues that might yet exist. Then, toward the end of the fifth day, Mr. Whittaker walked into J & J Outfitters and greeted Jonathan like an old friend.

"I'm sorry your grandfather's away," he said. "I've brought him a camera from Bangor, which I can return if it doesn't suit him. It was offered at a reasonable price. He needn't pay for it until he's on his feet again. When is he returning?"

On the verge of saying that Grandpa might be gone another few days, Jonathan blurted, "Soon, very soon." It seemed better to let Mr. Whittaker think that. Was it to keep the pressure on him, or was it for protection?

Mr. Whittaker said he would have left the camera upstairs, only the door was locked.

Carefully refraining from saying whether or not he had a key to the gallery door, Jonathan said the camera would be safe behind the counter here in the shop.

Mr. Whittaker hesitated. "Perhaps when I pick up the prints—"

"They're at Mrs. Noone's," Jonathan said. "Can you come for them after five?"

"Certainly." Mr. Whittaker lifted a box onto the counter. "Take care," he said, his hands still grasping the bulky package. "It survived the stage journey with me, but of course a camera is a fragile instrument."

Receiving the box, Jonathan noticed a bandage around Mr. Whittaker's wrist.

Mr. Whittaker caught Jonathan's glance and said, "I inflicted more of an injury on myself than I realized when we cleaned up after the accident."

"Is it better now?" Jonathan inquired politely.

"Thank you, yes. But that broken glass cut deep. It got nasty over the next day or so. I had to seek medical assistance."

Jonathan said no more, satisfied that there was a doctor who would be able to describe the injury he'd treated.

When the store closed, Jonathan headed straight for home. The test he hoped to apply would be more effective if Mr. Whittaker was unaware of Jonathan's suspicion. He wondered whether he would be clever enough to figure out whether Mr. Whittaker had been alerted.

Then Fred Whittaker came striding toward the house, whistling and at ease. His friendliness, like his anticipation, seemed genuine. "At long last," he exclaimed as Jonathan, heaving a secret sigh of relief, opened the door to the shed.

Mr. Whittaker carried the three photographs out into the light. "Ah," he said, sounding pleased. "Good. Very good. Too bad this one doesn't show logs coming."

Jonathan said, "There will be more. Grandpa didn't have time to print them all."

"Well, this is a nice start," Mr. Whittaker declared with convincing delight.

For an instant Jonathan worried that things were going too smoothly. Then he made his move. "There was one other," he said, "but it wouldn't do for an advertisement."

"Why is that?" Mr. Whittaker asked, still perusing the photographs.

"Grandpa had just turned the camera toward the rapids. The barn roof was coming. A bit of it shows in the picture, but not the whole thing. And way up in the corner there's someone with an overturned boat." Jonathan paused, telling himself to slow down, give Mr. Whittaker time to react.

Mr. Whittaker said, "When you told me about the barn roof, I thought it might make a good subject. Remember?"

Jonathan nodded. "There will be better pictures of the whole roof. They just aren't printed yet."

"Still," Mr. Whittaker said with just a hint of urgency, "I wouldn't mind deciding for myself what will and won't do. I'll just have a look at that print, too, then," he told Jonathan. "If it's no trouble," he added.

Jonathan stepped back into the shed and began to hunt. He took his time, opening and closing boxes and raising trays to peer beneath them. When the dim light inside the shed darkened, he knew that Mr. Whittaker was standing in the doorway. Still searching, Jonathan began to shake his head. "I wonder," he said without turning to face Mr. Whittaker, "whether Grandpa might have taken it with him. He likes to give people copies of pictures he's taken of them. Maybe he knows the man who was in that picture."

"But where was he going?" demanded Mr. Whittaker. "Up north again?"

"I'm not sure," Jonathan answered truthfully. "But he'll be here soon. You can speak to him then."

"Now that I'm here, why don't I help you look for it?" Mr. Whittaker suggested.

"No, thank you," Jonathan told him. "Grandpa doesn't want his things disturbed. I've already tried all the places I'm allowed to touch. You won't have long to wait."

By now Mr. Whittaker was standing in the middle of the shed, his eyes darting at shelves and chests. Jonathan, who finally faced him, tried to look calm and confident.

"I'll be at the inn as usual," Mr. Whittaker said. "Kindly inform me as soon as your grandfather arrives home." He strode out into the dimming light and walked rapidly away, his left hand waving irritably at the mosquitoes that pursued him.

Turning to close the door, Jonathan saw with a start of triumph that Mr. Whittaker had left the three river prints behind.

29

As soon as J & J Outfitters opened for business, Jonathan began to worry about being away from the house. Now that Mr. Whittaker had shown that what he was really after was the picture with the man, he didn't seem likely to return for the photographs left in the shed. But with Jonathan out of the way, he might continue his search for the missing print. Was it risky for Jonathan to carry on as though he hadn't an inkling that anything out of the ordinary was at stake? What if Mr. Firth spoke to Mr. Whittaker?

Jonathan supposed that Fergus Fearnaught or Wizard Will would prepare for any eventuality. But they were useless examples. The kind of big-city villainy they exposed was always recognizable. Here in Masham, a well-spoken gentleman could shield his despicable deeds with convincing civility.

Jonathan kept glancing anxiously at the door. But it was Annie, not Fred Whittaker, who stormed into the store. Flushed and breathless, she jabbered at him to hurry, hurry home this very minute.

Jonathan said, "What are you doing here? Where is every-one?"

"Come on. I'll explain," she told him. She waved to Ernie. "Ma wants Jonathan. All right?" She didn't wait for a reply. She all but dragged Jonathan outside.

"Did something happen to Grandpa?" he asked, running beside her as she pushed her bicycle up the road.

"In a way. It's happening right now. You'll never believe what we discovered."

"I thought you were going to stay with your grand-mother," he said.

"Not after what we found out. We came home as fast as we could. And guess what? Just now, the very moment we arrived, Uncle Rodney caught Mr. Whittaker in the shed." She paused, breathless. "Jonathan, you were right about him. We know why he wanted those pictures. It all fell into place, just like in *Honest Harry*."

"I found out, too, only I don't have enough proof yet," Jonathan told her. "I think he killed the Indian, the man they call Muskrat Mac."

Annie stopped so short he nearly knocked her down. "That's it!" she cried. "Mr. Whittaker must think Mac Nichols is dead, too. I have to make sure Uncle Rodney doesn't let on that he's alive."

"Alive?" Jonathan exclaimed.

"He's with some of Granny's relatives, recovering from a terrible ordeal." She thrust the bicycle at him and ran ahead, leaving him to push it up the hill.

As soon as Jonathan turned onto Orchard Road, he jumped on the bicycle and pedaled as hard as he could.

Annie and her mother were outside the house, head to

head. Ruby was still hitched to the buggy, parcels and bags strewn beside it. The shed door stood open.

"Annie," Jonathan blurted, "you said I was right about Mr. Whittaker. But I can't be right. I thought he killed Muskrat Mac. If Muskrat Mac's alive, I got it all wrong."

"Ssh!" Mrs. Noone raised a finger to her lips. Then in an undertone she said, "We'll explain later, Jonathan."

Grandpa appeared in the shed doorway and said calmly, "There you are, Jonathan. Did things go well these past few days?" Then he addressed Annie. "May I send you on one more errand, my dear? Mr. Whittaker here says Mr. Firth will be able to settle a misunderstanding we're having. Please ask that gentleman to join us."

"He's not at home," Fred Whittaker added from inside the shed. "He's at the mill in his office."

"Can't I stay?" Annie implored. "I'll miss—"

Her mother picked up the bicycle. "I'll do it," she said.

That brought Grandpa out to her. She whispered a few words to him, and he turned to Annie. "You can out-race your mother, you know. Why don't you go?"

Annie heaved an enormous sigh and took off just as Mr. Whittaker emerged from the shed.

"Ask your grandson," he said to Grandpa. "He'll tell you I forgot to take those pictures with me."

"If they were just where you left them," Grandpa asked, "why did you have to ransack the place?"

Jonathan walked over to the doorway and looked in. The shed was in shambles. "I just cleaned up here," he couldn't help exclaiming.

"I know what you think," Mr. Whittaker said to him. "Mr. Firth told me the outrageous story you concocted."

He turned toward Grandpa. "He also assured me that you consider those scurrilous charges the product of a schoolboy's inflamed fancy. I'm shocked that you take any of them seriously."

"I'm shocked, too," Grandpa replied. "I never expected to find you alone here treating my belongings like trash."

"It can be set to rights," Mr. Whittaker told him. "Rodney, I'm not your enemy. I've brought you a camera from Bangor. This is just a misunderstanding."

Jonathan went outside. Clouds were gathering. Thunder rumbled in the distance. "Shouldn't we carry in your things before they're rained on?" he asked Mrs. Noone. He picked up a carpetbag and a basket.

Mrs. Noone followed him into the house. When she had set down her box, she said quietly, "I assume you hid the other picture."

Jonathan nodded. "It's here in—"

"Never mind. Annie's right. That man needs to think it may supply some damning evidence. What about the other glass plates?"

"In Grandmother's shed. Underneath her basket strips."

"Well done," she said. "If he tries to squirm out of this, we'll have him anyway."

"I don't understand," Jonathan said.

"It was hard for us, too, even with the facts staring us in the face. When we first met Mac Nichols, your grandfather had no idea he was the Indian the lumbermen had spoken of. We left Annie with her granny for a couple of days, then returned to pick her up or to say good-bye for the summer. By then Annie had made the connection."

"Annie did?" Jonathan wasn't sure whether he was more

envious than impressed that Annie had cracked the case. "How did she figure it out?"

"Bit by bit," Mrs. Noone told him. "She heard about Mr. Nichols's misfortune, and it matched what you had told her. So we listened to his account, how he was going to leave the Fish Hawk Lake area when he heard that an ignorant newcomer, a young man who couldn't know the task was too treacherous for one person, had taken his place on the logjam. Mr. Nichols turned back, but the man was already in the river, barely alive. Even so, Mr. Nichols took a boat out to him, but logs caught it, slammed it onto rocks, turned it over on him, and split it open."

"Open?" Jonathan thought back to that morning. He couldn't recall seeing the boat split apart.

"Mr. Nichols said it happened in an instant. He saw the gap, reached for it, and it closed on his hand. He couldn't let go. With his fingers jammed in it, he couldn't free himself or even see more than water and logs and eventually a man's boots. That was when he heard what he guessed was someone with a peavey stabbing at logs jammed against the boat. Then it spun around, and he was carried down the rapids and miles farther. He managed to keep his head up, that's all, but his body was battered, and his fingers were crushed."

It was sickening for Jonathan to realize that while he had gaped at the river scene, a man had been trapped beneath the boat. "I never saw him," he whispered.

Mrs. Noone nodded. "No doubt. Mr. Nichols said he saw only the boots of the man with the peavey who came after him. He guessed it was Fred Whittaker."

"And now he knows?"

"Now we all know," Mrs. Noone said.

After the rest of the baggage was unloaded, Jonathan and Mrs. Noone unhitched Ruby and took her to her stall. By the time she was watered and rubbed down, Annie was back and Mr. Firth's carriage had drawn up behind the buggy.

30

Mrs. Noone invited everyone into the parlor. She even offered her visitors a cool drink of barley water flavored with raspberry juice. Jonathan and Annie passed around the glasses and then stood back, listening and watching.

Mr. Firth took charge of the discussion. His manner showed that he was accustomed to bringing people together to work out their difficulties. All these wrinkles would submit to the iron, he said.

Grandpa let him speak on until he seemed to have run out of things to say. Then he invited Mr. Whittaker to state his case. But all Fred Whittaker said was that when he came to fetch the prints he'd left behind, he had acted impulsively. His excuse was that he had just learned about Jonathan's charges and was anxious to clear himself.

Grandpa took a long drink of his raspberry water. Then he spoke. "At first I thought my grandson's accusation was reckless and farfetched. Thanks to the camera, as well as other evidence, I now know otherwise."

"What other evidence?" Fred Whittaker demanded. "I've done nothing."

"All in good time," Grandpa told him. "It grieves me to speak of such calamities, but unless you're prepared to admit your part in them, I must."

Huge raindrops spattered the window, stopped, and then began to drive more steadily against the house.

Grandpa said, "I'll begin with Muskrat Mac trapped beneath the boat."

"Wait!" Mr. Whittaker thrust out his arm. "That wasn't my doing. I tried to save him. Those narrow boats are slippery with wet pitch. There's no keel to grab."

"But you managed to shift the boat with a peavey," Grandpa continued, "and it went over the rapids. Like the young man Mac Nichols found in the river."

"It wasn't like that," Fred Whittaker protested. "I went to check, to be sure the logjam was cleared. When I saw the boat in with the logs, I knew something was wrong. Then I saw the hand. Not a whole hand. Fingers. I grabbed the peavey that was on the bank and I went out on logs as far as I dared. I tried to pry the boat free, to turn it up. But the water forced the logs against it. When I finally shoved off two of them, the current took the boat right out from under."

"So," said Grandpa, "instead of halting the coming run of logs to attempt a rescue, you threw Mac Nichols's gear sack in after him. You wanted the river drivers and woodsmen to think that he had taken his belongings and walked away. You didn't want them to know that you had sent those two men to their deaths."

"I had no idea the young man had gone down," Fred

Whittaker retorted. "I couldn't even be sure who was under the boat, though I guessed the Indian. Anyhow, there were other lives to think of. It was too late to stop the logs. The men had orders to open the boom and release them. Then the roof showed up. I knew it could block the run. There was barely time to clear the way. What else could I have done?"

Grandpa didn't answer. The rain drummed, and the parlor filled with an eerie darkness.

Mr. Firth said, "It may have been all, all you could have done, Fred. It's unfortunate, though, that you didn't report the accident."

"The accident, as you call it," said Grandpa, "was the result of a foolhardy decision. The job Fred expected a solitary man to do—first the Indian, then, when he refused, the boy—required at least two boats and maybe half a dozen men. The loggers knew that. They knew the river was running too fast. Fred knew next to nothing, and he wasn't willing to learn from those who did."

Neither man responded.

"Do you want to see the photograph now?" asked Grandpa.

"What's the point?" Mr. Firth declared. "Fred doesn't dispute what the camera recorded. It's a question of interpretation. I say, put an end to this sorry episode."

"Right," Grandpa agreed. "Of course that involves compensation."

Mr. Firth looked startled. "Surely Fred didn't cause the accident."

"Which accident?" Mrs. Noone inquired. She wore a puzzled frown. "There are two accidents, are there not? Two that you think he didn't cause."

Mr. Firth drew up his small frame. "They're not alike," he declared indignantly. "One is an act of nature; the other a brutal prank. Loggers and drivers take risks and lose limbs and lives. We can't support their families ever after. Besides, it's known that most Indian river drivers take liberties."

"The men who worked with Mac Nichols knew him as a good riverman."

Mr. Firth waved off Grandpa's remark and continued. "I wouldn't doubt that the Indian who came to grief there dug his own grave. And there is nothing to suggest that Fred had anything to do with your loss, Mr. Capewell."

"Perhaps Whittaker would like to offer a different answer?" Grandpa suggested.

Fred Whittaker sank back in his chair, his hand to his chin as if to stroke a beard that wasn't there. He shook his head.

"Ask him about his wrist," Jonathan whispered loudly.

"That was a glass cut," Fred Whittaker responded without much conviction.

Jonathan stared at him, seeking in that bland expression some hint of the person behind it. "Find out which doctor treated it," Jonathan said.

"All right, then," Fred Whittaker snapped, lurching to his feet. "So it was a burn." He moved to the window and swung around to face them. "Things got away from me. I meant no harm. I'd no idea the firecrackers would do more than singe the horse."

"What!" Mr. Firth exclaimed. "Fred, are you saying you committed that vile act?"

"It's not like that," Fred Whittaker insisted, appealing to Mr. Firth. "It's what you said, how it's interpreted. Once I'd heard the men saying that the roof had been photographed at the rapids, I knew the pictures could show more. I made every effort to get them. I never wanted to hurt the horse, but I was at my wit's end. The damage must have been from the firecrackers I stuck inside his surcingle. I thought they'd boost the one I threw at him to make him bolt. All I wanted was to lay that whole river incident to rest."

"Lay it to rest?" Mrs. Noone said. "You didn't think the two men would be found?"

"Well, yes, eventually. That's just it. I knew I wasn't responsible, but I could see how it looked. I had to get those photographs before people started asking questions."

"Weren't there bound to be questions anyway?" asked Grandpa.

"Yes, of course. But I thought I might avoid any connection with what happened at the logjam. I didn't want to have to defend my actions to the loggers, who always take sides. I have a business to run up their way. Those men can hold a grudge, even if it's only an Indian they think was wronged. I can't afford that. So when I couldn't get the river pictures, I did what I could to help myself. That's the truth, Rodney."

As quickly as it had come, the storm abated. Pale, watery light filtered through the window. As he stood with his back to it, Fred Whittaker's bland features seemed to dissolve in shadow.

"So you helped yourself to Teddy," Grandpa concluded softly.

Fred Whittaker started toward him, then drew back. "I expected the horse would run wild for a bit and upset things in the wagon. Since I'd be the first one on the scene, I could make sure the glass plates would never give me problems. That's what I intended, but things went awry. I'm sorry."

Mr. Firth rubbed his hands together. "Poor beast," he murmured to no one in particular. He avoided looking at Fred Whittaker. Then he spoke to Grandpa. "I suppose you can settle this through lawyers, or just between yourselves. Or," he added, "you can bring charges and take this miserable case to court."

"I've been thinking it over," Grandpa said. "Also, I've had sound advice from a wise bystander, Grandmother Noone. She thinks Mr. Whittaker needs to deal with the damage to Mac Nichols and his family. She's come up with what sounds like a just settlement for Mac. You see, he survived."

"Survived!" Fred Whittaker exclaimed. "He's alive?"

"Alive to tell the tale," Mrs. Noone informed him. "Despite the punishment dealt his body."

"Alive," Fred Whittaker repeated wonderingly, shaking his head. "How?"

Annie said, "Mr. Nichols believes he wasn't supposed to die that way. He told us he was meant to live, no matter how badly he got hurt. He says that if a man is born to be drowned, a mud puddle in the middle of the road is deep enough to do it."

"I should think you'd be overjoyed to learn you hadn't killed him," Mrs. Noone remarked coolly.

"I didn't—" Mr. Whittaker began to protest. Then he fixed her with a look of sullen rage and shut his mouth, the mask of blandness for once stripped from his face.

Grandpa continued. "Some of Mac Nichols's fingers were crushed so badly that he'll never work as a logger again. But he knows the north woods from Old Town to St. John and would make an excellent guide for your wilderness tours. That's one wise woman's solution then: guaranteed work at fair wages. I'll be glad to handle the agreement, but you will have to meet with Mr. Nichols from time to time. I hope you'll be able to look him in the eye."

Fred Whittaker's eyes turned to stones. The mask was restored, shielding him from them all. And doubtless shielding him from himself as well, thought Jonathan. Could a camera penetrate that mask? he wondered. Could a photograph expose the true Fred Whittaker or even hint at the man who had, for an instant, bared himself?

Mr. Firth said to Grandpa, "What about compensation for you?"

"I'll want replacements where possible," Grandpa told him. "My horse, Teddy, being irreplaceable, I need time to figure out how I'm to get along without him. I'm some old to start a young horse. Teddy knew my ways; I knew his. We were partners."

Mr. Firth rose and walked to the door, passing Fred Whittaker without so much as a glance his way. Outside, everything steamed as the July sun bore down through the drenched trees. Mr. Firth's horse glistened from the rain.

"I wonder who lost most this day," Grandpa murmured, watching the two men disappear separately down Orchard Road.

Mrs. Noone went to stand beside him. When they turned back to the house, they smiled at Annie and Jonathan in the doorway.

"Can you bear to hear more news?" Mrs. Noone asked them. Then, without waiting for a reply, she said, "Rodney and I were married last Wednesday."

"What!" exclaimed Annie. "Behind my back?"

"Well, after we left you with your granny."

"How could you?" Annie cried.

"How indeed?" Mrs. Noone replied. "These are among life's great mysteries."

"Don't ask me," Grandpa said. "I can't even understand why one person risks the life of another, let alone how two people dare to cast their lot together."

"But what now?" Jonathan blurted, wondering how he could face his family. They had counted on him to keep this from happening.

"Now?" said Grandpa. "I say a good meal is called for. And maybe another bottle of raspberry juice?"

31

Just before sunrise on a cool Sunday morning in late August they set off for a visit to the farm. Grandpa had written a proper letter, which he'd read aloud at breakfast before sending it, to see if his Masham family thought it would pass muster.

"Dear children," it began.

"Maybe you should say you mean the grown-up ones," Annie suggested.

Her mother told her to hush and listen.

"It has been a busy summer," the letter continued, "and you will learn of it soon, as we are coming next Sunday and will stay to dinner if you will have us. Miranda is bringing a maple cake. Jonathan has a special camera of his own now. It is called a detective camera, since he has shown some bent in that direction. He hopes you are well and looks forward to being home."

"Is that true?" asked Annie.

Jonathan wasn't sure. "If I can come back here again," he said.

Grandpa said, "Let Miranda and me take the lead with that question."

Even with Ruby trotting along smartly, it took almost four hours to reach the village. Annie asked the names of everyone in each house. Suddenly Jonathan wondered whether he would have time to see Warren. If Mama and Dad let him live in Masham, then when school started, he would finally get to know some of the town boys. Even Annie admitted that they weren't all mean. But no one could take Warren's place.

Rose had been waiting for them. When he saw her waving, he couldn't contain his excitement, and Grandpa had to tell him to sit back down until the buggy stopped. But the moment Simon, squinting and grinning, stepped out of the dark barn into the midday glare, Jonathan jumped to the ground. Then Dad and Albert came around from the woodshed. Mama, the last to appear, emerged from the house, wiping her hands on her apron.

Rose hugged Grandpa and Jonathan. That eased the first awkward moments. Dad was so pleased to see his father and his youngest child that his welcome spilled over to include the new guests. Only Mama, who made an effort to sound cordial, couldn't conceal her wariness. Jonathan was surprised at how old she looked next to Annie's mother.

Grandpa didn't break the marriage news until dinner was nearly over. Then he said, "This is the nearest we've come to having a wedding cake, Miranda and I." His announcement produced a stunned silence.

He plunged on. "It has seemed for some time that my life was in Masham and on the road." He spoke directly to his son. "It's where my living is, just as this farm is your living.

I've been increasingly useless here. I need to make a change while I can still do something with my remaining years."

Dad nodded. Still, he didn't seem to know what to say.

"When I first began to work in Masham, Justin and Miranda Noone befriended me. When Annie came along, I shared their joy, and when Justin passed away, I shared Miranda's sorrow. Despite many differences, we have formed a bond. I hope ours will be an equal partnership, but so far I'm overly indebted to her."

Annie's mother broke in. "That's Rodney's point of view, and I don't hold to it, except in minor ways, like overriding his objections and rescuing some of his best photographs. Not too long ago, I sent them off to the Photography Academy of America because Rodney wouldn't be bothered. One of them has won a prize, and three are to be shown in a gallery in New York City."

This disclosure broke the dam of silence. Everyone except Mama began to speak at once.

Annie's mother told them she was still trying to convince Rodney to travel to New York in October to receive the award. "Ordinarily Annie's grandmother would be in Masham, but this year she expects to stay with relatives until the end of that month. We could take the stage to Bangor and the train from Bangor to Boston and then the steamer to New York. If the children could stay with you," Annie's mother added. "They would miss only a week or so of school."

Silence swept across the table as the import of this request sank in. Jonathan held his breath. Annie's mother had slipped up and forced the issue too soon. Now it was up to Grandpa to smooth things over.

Grandpa finished his slice of maple cake before speaking. Probably he was figuring out how best to make his case. Had there really been a time, Jonathan wondered, when he questioned whether Grandpa had all his wits about him?

Finally Grandpa pushed his chair back, raised his eyebrows at Annie's mother, complimented her on her excellent baking, and launched into a plea for Jonathan. First he spoke of the progress the boy was making, then how photography could give him a living. Then he mentioned the opportunity to take his education farther in the Masham school. After that Grandpa referred to his own problems caused by advancing age. Facing Jonathan's mother, he said, "I confess I was reluctant to take on my youngest grandson. But, Sara, you were right. Just as you promised when you urged me to accept the arrangement, it's proved a benefit to us both."

At this point the younger family members were excused from the table. Rose took Annie upstairs. Simon beckoned to Jonathan, and they went out to the cool barn.

"You were supposed to watch him," Simon said.

"I did. I let him out of my sight just once. Anyway, what difference does it make? He doesn't want to live here. Neither does she. She owns a whole store. It was Annie's grandfather's store first and then her father's. Now Mrs. Noone runs it. I mean, Aunt Miranda. The photograph gallery is above it. Their house is nice, too. And now that Grandpa's moved in there, I have my own separate room over the wood-house. And the wood for the stove is delivered already chopped."

"Is Annie adopted? She's not fair like her mother."

"No. Her grandfather was married to an Indian woman."

"Oh." Simon thought for a moment. "Do you want to stay with them?"

"In a way," Jonathan answered. "So much has changed. It feels as though I've been there a long time. Town is different. I know I'll miss you and the others. It's complicated there. More noise and more things and more money. But that's not what matters." How could he explain without telling Simon what had happened?

"What does matter then?" Simon asked.

Jonathan drew a deep breath. "Not what I used to think. Annie is the one who wants to be a detective now. She's taken to my dime novels, and she's full of notions from them. See, I want to take pictures of people who aren't posing, who don't know that I'm photographing them, but not to solve crimes. I want my camera to catch the looks on people's faces that tell you what they're thinking and feeling, who they really are. Some people wear masks. I want to make pictures that won't be fooled by them."

Simon said, "You have changed, little brother."

"I didn't mean to," Jonathan answered. Then he added, "Annie's grandmother doesn't trust any camera. She thinks it'll steal her soul, what she calls her shadow spirit. I think she's partly right and partly wrong. It can't rob a person of her self. But it can capture that self. That's what I need to learn how to do."

Rose and Annie joined them in the barn.

"I'd love to spend a week here," Annie said as they peered over a stall door at two wobbly calves. "Do you think Mrs. Capewell will ever get to like me?"

Simon said, "Give her time. Show her you enjoy being here. That should do it."

Rose said, "I'll tell her how glad I am, since I've always wanted a sister."

"Only Annie's more like a cousin," Jonathan pointed out.

"Oh, no!" Annie informed him. "When Ma married Uncle Rodney, I became your aunt. I think."

They all argued amiably over the nature of this new relationship and then swapped stories about when they were little.

By the time Ruby was harnessed and hitched, Jonathan could sense a change in the climate. It felt as though the ice was finally breaking up, the water rising, the family logjam floating free.

This thaw seemed to him like the breath of a new season. Maybe now the river would flow without hindrance all the way to Masham.